Sign up for our newsletter to hear
about new releases, read interviews with
authors, enter giveaways, and more.

http://www.ylva-publishing.com

Other Books by this Author

Coming Home
Broken Faith
Walking the Labyrinth
Kicker's Journey

Bitter Fruit
A LESBIAN ROMANCE

Lois Cloarec Hart

Acknowledgements

Converting and expanding my 2001 novella, *The Lion and the Lamb*, to this novel, *Bitter Fruit*, wasn't originally on my writing schedule, though that imaginary document is never written in stone. It frequently contorts with whimsy and convolutes with woe. But when my publisher, Astrid Ohletz, suggested that *Lion* would lend itself to a larger story, I took on the project with the help of my wonderful long-time collaborators, Day Petersen and Kathleen Grams-Gibbs. I was writing *The Lion and the Lamb* when Day and I first met over thirteen years ago, and my now-wife has worked on everything I've written since. My dear friend, Kathy, came on board a few years later, and between the two of them, they make our collaborations joyful endeavours. My deepest thanks to you both.

I'm also very grateful to Astrid for her concept and support; to Alissa McGowan for her skilled first edit; and to Ylva's senior editor, Sandra Gerth, for her steadfast encouragement and insightful second edit. Glendon, as usual, your covers are works of art.

For Day

Whose quips make me laugh,
Whose songs make me cry,
Whose love makes me soar.

Chapter 1

"I'm bored."

Uh-oh. Victoria glanced at Jac, whose restless gaze swept the bar, stopping occasionally to scan a knot of people or linger on a woman sitting alone.

Victoria sighed. *I should've stayed home tonight.* "You were the one who talked me into a girls' night out."

"Roger's out of town. There was no point in you sitting home all alone."

"But did it have to be The Arc?"

"What's wrong with The Arc? The music is good, drinks are reasonable…" Jac's gaze followed a woman walking past them. "The women are fine. What's not to like?"

The fact that I'm really tired of being your wingwoman. "Just once I'd like to go to a regular bar. Just once. Why couldn't we try Marco's on Seventeenth?"

"Marco's? You're married and I'm gay. If we go to Marco's, neither of us are getting lucky tonight. At least here…" She winked.

"Yeah, yeah, I know. Here you can walk up to just about any woman and find a cure for your ennui." Victoria rolled her eyes.

"Just about? You doubt me, old friend?"

Victoria groaned, dropped her head on the bar, and thumped it a few times. "God forbid that I ever doubt Jac the Invincible, Jac the Seductress, Jac the Temptress, Jac the mphhh—"

"Okay, I get your point." Jac laughed and removed her hand from Victoria's mouth.

"You are such an arrogant bitch."

"True, but you love me." Jac sipped her drink, surveying the room.

"So, what's the matter? Don't see anyone to your liking tonight?"

"Aw, I don't know. Maybe I'm not in the mood or something. Jesus, Vic, look at them."

Victoria glanced over her shoulder. "What's the matter with them?"

Jac sighed, turned her back to the crowd, and signaled the bartender for another round. "Nothing, really. Awfully vanilla, though. Hell, they'd probably go running to Mommy if I turned one of them over my knee."

"Well, if that's the problem, why don't you go to Sous-terre?" The ultra-secretive private club was notorious for catering to those with darker sexual tastes, and though Victoria had never been there, Jac was a frequent patron.

Jac continued to stare at the bottles lined up behind the bar, her expression unreadable.

"Maybe later." She threw some bills on the bar, then downed half the Scotch in one swallow. "There's no challenge anymore. Not here, not at Sous-terre. Nowhere."

Victoria scowled. "It's not like you can have absolutely any woman you want, you know."

Jac's eyebrow rose. "Is that a challenge?"

Victoria froze, and a cold sweat broke out on her forehead. When she failed to respond, Jac smirked and looked away.

Suddenly Victoria wanted nothing so much as to win a round from her charismatic friend. Jac had always been the alpha female in their friendship, and as much as Victoria loved her, she ached to claim the laurels at least once. She didn't allow for second thoughts. "Yes, it is."

Now both eyebrows rose, and Jac straightened. "Name your terms."

"I select the target. You have one month, exactly thirty-one days, to get her into bed or you lose." Victoria was nauseous, but she couldn't back down now.

"And the wager?"

Victoria hesitated. She had intended to bet money, but impulsively altered her conditions. "If you win, I'll talk Roger into us going to Sous-terre with you."

Jac tilted her head. "I didn't think you had any interest in the club, but all right. And if you win? Not that there's a chance you will, mind you."

Victoria clenched her hands around her martini glass and refused to meet Jac's gaze. "If I win, you forget about your rules and lines of demarcation, and come to the mountains with me for a whole weekend."

There was a sharp intake of breath.

Victoria finally forced herself to look up.

Jac's expression was grave. "That really doesn't sound like a good idea. Do you understand the risks? We've been partway down this path before and it didn't work out well for any of us."

Victoria was acutely aware that what she was proposing had the potential to destroy their friendship and her marriage. Jac had always been adamantly against crossing that line, but Victoria was helpless to resist a chance, however remote, to be with the only woman who haunted her erotic dreams. "That's the deal. Take it or leave it." *Dr. Eichler would have my head if he could hear me, but I don't care.*

Long moments passed, until Victoria became sure that her challenge would be refused.

"You're on, but only because I know you're going to lose."

Victoria exhaled deeply and her hands trembled. She didn't know whether to celebrate or pass out.

Jac focused a cool, businesslike gaze on Victoria. "So who's the target?"

"Her name is Lauren Blaine. She's a young woman I work with at the agency."

"Tell me about her."

"She's a great kid. One of those people who has a real, deep down goodness to her, you know? As for looks, she's cute. She's not very tall, but you can tell she's in good shape. She's got short dark hair, kinda shaggy, and big innocent eyes that see right through you."

"So, what aren't you telling me?"

Victoria knew Jac wouldn't renege now that she had accepted the challenge, so, with a smile, she threw down her ace. "She's straight, and engaged to be married."

Jac shrugged. "Minor details. So, when and how do I meet her?"

"I'm taking her out to lunch on Monday for her twenty-fifth birthday. Why don't you meet us at The Aerie for lunch about one?"

"Done."

Victoria raised a finger. "And your thirty-one days start ticking off the moment you meet her."

"All right, but I have terms, too. You're not allowed to run me down to her, or say or do anything to influence the outcome of the bet. Agreed?"

"Agreed."

Jac pushed away from the bar. "I'll see you on Monday."

Victoria watched Jac prowl the crowded room. She wasn't the least bit surprised when Jac moved in on the women around the pool table and skillfully separated a curly haired blonde from the pack.

Jac leaned close, lightly running one finger down the woman's arm as she whispered to her. When the blonde laughed and wrapped an arm around Jac's waist, Victoria shook her head. "Here we go again." The evening ended in its usual precipitous manner when Jac and the other woman left the bar shortly thereafter.

Why do I always do this to myself? I could turn down her invitations. I don't have to say yes. She sighed. *Get real. You'll take being with her any way you can, and you know it.*

People were Jac's friends on Jac's terms. If they didn't accept that, she made no effort to try to change their minds. No one, friend or lover, ever truly pierced her impassive exterior. Part of Victoria's sexual obsession was a desire to see if Jac even let herself go in the throes of passion. *That, and the fact that you know she'd twist you in knots and wring you inside out.*

Exasperated with herself, Victoria banished that line of thinking and contemplated the wager. She had a minor crisis of conscience about turning a wolf loose on the vulnerable young woman with whom she shared an office, but Lauren was devoted to her fiancé. All she talked about was house hunting and planning their life together. *She's way too committed to fall for Jac.*

Banishing any ethical qualms, Victoria pushed her empty glass across the bar and shook her head at the bartender. She twisted her wedding ring several times on her finger as her conscience pricked her. *I didn't do anything wrong.*

As she left the bar, she tried hard to stop imagining what Jac and the blonde were up to. She failed.

"I called a cab for you. It'll be waiting downstairs. I've already taken care of the fare." Jac held out the woman's coat and purse.

"I can stay, you know. I don't have to hurry home."

Yes, you do. "I have to be up very early for another engagement and it wouldn't be fair to you to roust you out of here at five o'clock in the morning."

"All right." The woman took a card from her purse and scrawled on the back. "Here's my number. I had fun tonight, and I'd love to do it again some time."

"It was wonderful, wasn't it? Are you okay going down by yourself or would you like me to walk you?" *Please say no.*

The woman leaned close and slipped her hand inside Jac's gown to fondle her breasts. "If you walk me down, we might not make it outside."

Jac fought to stop herself from flinching. She gently but firmly removed the woman's hand, taking it between hers. "As lovely as that sounds, I really need to get some sleep tonight."

"Your loss."

"Indeed. Take care of yourself, and thank you again for this evening."

"My pleasure." The woman waved and left the loft.

Jac locked the door, leaned against it, and closed her eyes. "Remind me again why I thought that was a good idea?" She turned off the lights and walked to her windows, where she watched her latest conquest get into the taxi. When the car drove away, she lifted her gaze to the cityscape, bright with lights across the river. *Are there any truly happy people out there?*

She glanced at the clock. 12:07. *I wonder if Marc's still up. It's not even midnight his time.* Jac picked up the phone and hit the speed dial for her brother, but the call went straight to voice mail. She ended it without leaving a message.

For a long moment she stared at the receiver, trying to think who else might help ease the profound melancholy that shrouded her thoughts.

No one. If you took Marc and Victoria out of the picture, there wasn't a single soul she could call in the midnight hours. God, how pathetic.

With a weary shake of her head, she set the phone down and turned to climb the stairs back to her bedroom.

Chapter 2

Lauren glanced at Phillip, who was totally focused on a tiny screen. He hadn't looked up from his smartphone since they'd left the city. "Everyone's really looking forward to meeting you. Mom's making a big Sunday dinner, and she asked me what your favourites were."

Phil grunted without looking up.

"Courtney, Adam, and Anjali couldn't make it down from Edmonton, but I think everyone else will be there."

"Trying to watch the game here, babe."

Lauren sighed. He wouldn't even say hi when she and her mother Skyped. It had taken months to convince him to go home with her to meet her family. "Please make an effort, hon. These are going to be your in-laws, after all—the grandparents of our children."

He sighed and lowered his phone. "I'm going, aren't I? I gave up three games this afternoon." The roar of a crowd rose from his phone, and he snatched it up. "Yes! Touchdown!"

Uh-huh, you gave up the games all right. Lauren shook her head and focused on the road. The narrow, straight lane ran between fields that were golden in the early September sunlight. Her heart rate picked up as she spotted the Andersons' distinctive barn-shaped mailbox. Five minutes to home. She hadn't made the trip from the city since mid-August, and she could hardly wait to see her family. *Phil and Jason should get along well. They're both sports crazy.*

When Lauren turned into the long driveway, her mother and brother were in the front yard watching two small boys pick up windfalls under the apple trees. "Oh good, Brian and Andrea made it. You'll love my nephews. They're adorable." She waved at her mother and slowed as her nephews ran toward the car.

"Who's the dude in the wheelchair?" Phil asked.

"That's my brother, Zac. He's got cerebral palsy."

"He's black."

"So? I've told you six of my siblings are adopted."

Phil shot her a frown. "Yeah, but you never said one of 'em was black."

"And one sister is East Indian and one has Down's, so what? They're my family. That's all that matters." Lauren parked her car next to two pickup trucks, turned off the engine, and hopped out. She swept Jacob and Nick into her arms, laughing as they smothered her with wet kisses.

"Did you bring us something, Auntie Laurie?" Jacob asked.

"Bring, bring, bring," Nick echoed.

Lauren managed to get a hand into her jacket pocket and came up with two Tootsie Pops. "Something like this, you mean?" She grinned at their squeals of delight.

"Come on, you two, let your auntie catch her breath." Lauren's mother pried three-year-old Nick out of her arms. "Go tell your daddy that his little sister is here."

Five-year-old Jacob squirmed to break free of Lauren's embrace. "Me too, me too! I want to go tell Daddy, too."

She laughed and set him down to chase after his brother.

Her mother used her apron to wipe Lauren's face. "Sorry about that. They were having such fun gathering pie apples for me that I couldn't say no when they wanted one to eat." She wrapped her arms around Lauren and hugged her. "It's so good to have you home. Happy almost birthday, Laurie."

"Thanks, Mom." Lauren turned to Phil and gestured him forward. "Mom, this is Phillip. Phil, this is my mom, Cynthia."

Phil shook her hand. "Nice to meet you."

"You too," Cynthia said. "We've been so looking forward to this." She patted Lauren's arm. "Why don't we go up to the house? You're probably thirsty after that long drive."

Lauren laughed. "It's only a couple of hours, Mom. I didn't exactly have to pack up the wagon train to make the trip."

Her mother chuckled and linked arms with Lauren. They walked up the pathway with Phil trailing behind.

"Is Dad working today?"

"He was, but he'll be in soon. He and Jason are finishing the last of the harvest. The rain last week delayed them, but your dad thinks it'll be a bumper crop this year."

"That's wonderful." Lauren stopped to kneel at Zac's side and hugged him gently. "Hey, sweetie. How's my favourite little brother?" She held steady while his arms jerked around her and he rested his head on her shoulder. "Mom said your new therapist is working wonders."

"She's a pistol all right, isn't she, Son?" Cynthia smiled at him.

Zac's eyes shone as he nodded.

Lauren rose and turned to Phil. "Phil, this is my brother, Zac." The door opened and Lauren grinned. "And this is my big brother, Brian, and his beautiful wife, Andrea."

Andrea laughed and shifted Nick to her other hip. "You are such a charmer. It's a wonder you've stayed single this long." She hugged Lauren and extended a hand to Phil. "We've heard so much about you. It's a pleasure to meet you at last."

"Thanks." Phil shook hands with Andrea and then Brian before an explosion of noise emanated from his phone, and he snuck a glance.

Lauren rolled her eyes. "Don't mind him. His Seahawks are playing. The world could come to an end, and he wouldn't notice."

"I've got the game on inside," Brian said. "You're welcome to join me."

"Awesome." Phil started to follow Brian, Jacob trailing behind them, when Sara came out of the door and immediately wrapped her arms around Phil. She giggled, jouncing him up and down.

He flinched and tried to pull free.

Lauren winced. She'd cautioned Phil about Sara's affectionate reaction to complete strangers. *I guess he forgot.*

"Sara, come say hi to your sister." Cynthia held out her hand.

Sara let go, and Phil bolted into the house.

Lauren exchanged hugs with Sara.

"See my new shoes, Laurie?"

"I do. They're beautiful." Lauren admired Sara's shoes as she lifted each foot up. "Did Mom help you choose them?"

"Unh-uh. I picked them out all by myself. Do you want to see my new coat? Mom helped me pick that out."

Lauren slung an arm around Sara's shoulders. "I'd love to see it."

After Lauren admired the additions to Sara's wardrobe and spent time with Zac, she went to find Phil, who was in the living room with Brian. "Would you like to come on a tour of the property, hon? It'll be a couple of hours until dinner—lots of time to show you all my favourite spots."

Never taking his eyes off the TV, Phil shook his head. "Maybe later, babe. The fourth quarter just started and the Seahawks are only down by three."

Lauren watched him for a moment, then turned away. "Guess I'll go help Mom."

Lauren leaned over to whisper in Phil's ear. "Please turn it off. Mom's rule is no phones at the dinner table."

He scowled, but muted the phone and put it in his pocket.

"So, Phil, Laurie tells us you work with your dad." Steven nodded at Jason. "I don't know how I'd run this place without my son. Your father must be thrilled that you joined the family business."

"I guess." Phil heaped more chicken onto his plate.

"There are branches of Emerson's Luxury Auto in Calgary, Lethbridge, and Edmonton now, Dad," Lauren said. "Phil was in sales, but he was promoted to management a few months ago, just after we got engaged. Frank—that's Phil's dad—says at the rate Phil's learning the ropes, he'll be able to take early retirement." *Okay, a little exaggeration, but what can it hurt?*

"If Phil is in luxury autos, why are you still driving that old bug?" Jason winked at her.

Phil snorted. "That's what I keep telling her. It's not good for our image when she runs around town in that bucket of bolts."

"It's not a bucket of bolts," Lauren said. "It's served me well since I left high school, and it deserves better than being thrown over for some fancy piece of tin."

Phil bristled. "Fancy piece of tin? I'm not asking you to drive a Porsche, for God's sake, but you could at least let me put you in a Lincoln or an Audi."

"Which you would sell right out from under me in a heartbeat if you found a buyer for it, so, no, thanks.

The Beetle may have a few miles on it, but it's mine and it's paid for."

"I like your yellow car," Sara said.

Lauren smiled. "Thanks, sweetie. I do, too." She glanced at her mother. Cynthia met her gaze for a moment, then turned to help Zac. *Damn it. No one's teasing. This isn't good.* Whenever one of her siblings brought someone home to meet the family, they were usually subjected to endless teasing. Everyone had been perfectly polite to Phil all afternoon, but not even Jason had cracked a joke.

After dinner, Lauren helped her mother clean up the kitchen.

Phillip poked his head around the doorjamb. "Can we get going, babe? I'm going to miss the second half of the night game if we don't leave now."

Lauren hung up her dish towel. "All right. I'll be there in a moment. Thanks very much for dinner, Mom. It was fabulous, as always."

"You're welcome. You're always welcome, you know that. Would you like to take a couple slices of pie home with you?"

"No, thanks. You save the rest. I know how much Jason and Sara love your pie."

"I made three pies, lots for everyone, though I do wish you'd let me make you a birthday cake. It just doesn't seem right not to have one when your big day is tomorrow."

"I appreciate it, Mom. I really do. But there was enough stress with introducing Phil to the family. I didn't want to add to the hassle."

"Phsst. As if celebrating any of your birthdays is ever anything but a pleasure."

Lauren hugged her mother. "Please don't worry about it. You made my favourite key lime pie and that's always a special treat."

"All right…but I do have some presents for you to take home, and don't even think of telling me no."

Lauren chuckled. "I wouldn't dream of it."

"Are you sure Phil wouldn't like another piece of pie for later?"

Lauren hesitated. Phil *had* eaten two slices at dinner. "If you're sure, you can spare one."

"I can." Cynthia busied herself slicing and wrapping a generous wedge.

"Mom?"

"Yes?" Cynthia met Lauren's plaintive gaze.

"You've been awfully quiet. Is everything all right?"

"Of course. I'm just a little preoccupied, that's all. I've got a lot on the schedule this week."

"I know, but…" Lauren wasn't sure she wanted to put her question into words.

Cynthia reached for Lauren and pulled her into a long hug. With a sigh, she finally released her. "I'm sure he'll grow on us, sweetie. All that matters is that you love him." She pressed her lips firmly together and handed Lauren the pie. "You make sure you stay in touch now, okay? Zac and Sara love to see you on Skype, and so do I. Makes me forget you're so far away in the big city."

"Between me, Courtney, Anjali, and Adam, you must spend half your time on Skype."

Cynthia laughed. "Not quite, and your brother isn't nearly as good as you and your sisters about staying in touch, but it does liven up the evenings when you all call."

She walked Lauren to the front door where her family waited to share hugs and kisses.

Lauren glanced out at the car. Phil was already sitting in the passenger seat, his head down.

"You come back soon," Andrea said. "The boys miss their auntie."

"You mean they miss the Tootsie Pops." Lauren knelt and hugged the boys one last time. "You two be good, and I'll see what I can bring the next trip, okay?"

Cynthia pulled a brown grocery bag out of the closet and handed it to Lauren. There were several brightly wrapped packages inside.

"Thanks, Mom."

"I'll Skype you tomorrow evening, okay? I can't let your special day go by without singing to you."

Lauren nodded. "Looking forward to it." Her family followed her down the ramp to her car.

"We miss you," her father said. "Don't stay away too long."

Jason waved. "See you next time."

The drive home was quiet.

Phil was lost in his game.

Lauren was lost in her thoughts.

Chapter 3

Lauren looked up from the computer when Victoria stopped by her desk.

"Are we still on for lunch today, birthday girl?"

"That sounds wonderful. But you really don't have to treat. I'd be happy to pay my own way."

Victoria waved a dismissive hand. "Don't be silly. Of course it's my treat. It's your special day. But I did want to ask if you'd mind if an old friend of mine joins us."

"Of course not. Any friend of yours, and all that."

"Thanks. I should warn you that Jac can sometimes be a little overpowering. I think it's because she had to fight so hard to make it up the corporate ladder and it's hardened her a little. But she's got a good heart, and she and I go way back."

"No worries. I look forward to meeting her."

Victoria perched on the corner of her desk. "So, did Phil give you a birthday present yet?"

"Um, no. He never said anything this morning, but then he was running late and in such a hurry that he almost forgot his phone."

"Oh my God, not his phone. I'm sure he has romantic plans for later tonight."

"Maybe. Probably." *Hopefully.*

"How did it go with introducing him to your family this weekend? Did they think he was the best thing since sliced bread?"

"It went well, I think. You know how these things go—first meeting with the in-laws-to-be. People just need time to get to know each other, so it was a little stiff."

"I know exactly what you mean. The first time I met Roger's mother, I was so focused on being on my best behavior that I'm sure she thought he was engaged to a stick-in-the-mud."

Lauren laughed. "I can't even imagine you being a stick-in-the-mud."

"Neither could Roger's mother after the stagette party." Victoria winked and stood up. "Well, I'd best get back to work. I told Jac we'd meet her about one at The Aerie. Is that good for you? Irene and Janet said they'd cover for us."

"Sure, that sounds fine."

Jac glanced from the data on her computer screen to the time. She had forty-five minutes before she was to meet up with Victoria, and she needed to pick up the first element of her campaign.

Jac enjoyed the anticipation that curled within. Victoria's challenge had been completely unexpected but welcome. There weren't a lot of thrills left in her job.

Her earlier years with the bank had provided the stimulation of climbing the corporate ladder, and she had taken great satisfaction in advancing from being a freshly minted MBA to senior sales leader—commercial lending in record time. The men who once trained her now reported to her, a fact that occasioned some resentment in the lower echelons.

For the most part, she ignored the rumblings of discontent and muffled complaints of gender preference. At thirty-four, she had forged her career advancement much as a general would wage a military campaign— understanding her opponents, her allies, and the field of battle—with intimate savvy and unrelenting hard work. And of course, it helped to have no home life and no domestic commitments.

She sighed. In the past few months, her six-figure income, the downtown loft overlooking the river, and the perks her wealth and position brought her felt like small compensation for the loneliness that dogged her with increasing frequency. At least the bet was a break in her routine.

Jac wrenched her mind from its maudlin track. "All right. That's enough of that nonsense." She had an excellent job, terrific prospects, and an intriguing challenge to keep her attention for the next month. Once she had bedded Victoria's friend, she would turn serious attention to achieving the next level in management. "Jacqueline Lanier—Senior Executive. I like the sound of that."

Jac paused in the alcove of the restaurant. She spotted Victoria and another woman seated at a corner table and took a moment to study her prey. Vic hadn't lied. The woman was cute, in a girl-next-door kind of way.

Lauren had a slim, compact build and a sweet, open face with a healthy crop of freckles. Sunbeams danced off her chestnut hair, illuminating red highlights.

Jac spoke briefly to the maître d', handed her coat to the attendant, and began to make her way across the floor. She held a slim, paper-wrapped cylinder. *Did Vic say what colour her eyes are? I can't remember.* Jac prided herself on her excellent memory for details, and this challenge was going to demand the utmost from her intelligence, charm, and strategic skills.

Just then, Lauren looked up and met Jac's gaze, her big brown eyes sparkling with curiosity.

"Hello, Victoria." Jac extended her hand. "And you must be Lauren. I hope you don't mind me joining you. It's just been so long since I've been able to get together with my best friend that when I heard she was having lunch out today, I rather rudely invited myself."

There was genuine warmth in Lauren's gaze as she shook Jac's hand. "Not at all. You're most welcome. I've been looking forward to our meeting. Victoria speaks of you often."

Jac set the cylinder in front of Lauren. "This is a small apology for crashing your birthday celebration, as well as congratulations on the big day." She slid into the chair opposite Lauren, amused at the other woman's childlike delight with the surprise.

Lauren carefully peeled back the paper to reveal two perfect roses—one white and one red—in a tiny crystal bud vase.

"Oh, my heavens. These are beautiful. Aren't they beautiful, Victoria?"

"Yes. Jac's always had excellent taste."

Jac ignored Vic's acidic glance. "So, which birthday is it?"

"Twenty-fifth."

"A whole quarter century? Then this is an occasion for celebration. I hope your twenty-fifth year is filled with marvels, magic, and much joy."

Lauren looked up shyly. "It's certainly gotten off to a good start. Thank you very much." She ran a finger over the red rose, tracing the softness of the petals.

Struck by the unintended eroticism of the gesture, Jac took a hasty swallow of her water.

"We're ready to order," Victoria said. "You'd better catch up."

"Of course. I know we all have to get back to the office."

Once their orders were taken, menus collected, and coffee cups refilled, they resumed their conversation. Well aware that she was under scrutiny by both companions, Jac maintained an amiable expression, smiling often and chatting comfortably. Small talk did not come naturally to her, but she had trained herself in the art and it stood her in good stead in the corporate world. Now she used it to draw out her target. "Have you been working with Vic long, Lauren?"

"I've been at the agency for just over a year now. Victoria was wonderful about taking me under her wing and teaching me the trade." Lauren smiled at Victoria.

"Do you enjoy it?" Jac liked the sound of Lauren's voice, but reminded herself this was business, not pleasure. *Though if what's under that dress looks as good as I think it will, there's going to be a lot of pleasure involved too.*

"I love it. It's wonderful helping people plan their dream vacations and go places they've never been. And then there are all the business trips I take. I just got back from the Cook Islands last month. Do you like to travel?"

"I do enjoy it. However, a certain best friend, who shall remain nameless, sent me to this godforsaken island off India last year, where I'm convinced they still practice cannibalism." Jac grinned at Victoria.

"Hey, you're the one who said she wanted to get off the beaten path."

"Uh-huh. Off the beaten path, Vic, not on a whole other planet." Jac exulted in the sound of Lauren's laughter. *And we're off...*

They chatted easily as their meals were served, and time passed swiftly.

Jac was pondering her next move when Lauren laid a hand on Victoria's arm.

"Are you sure you can't come on Friday? I hate to waste the tickets, and I don't want to go alone."

Victoria shook her head. "Roger and I have been invited to his boss' place, and we really have to go."

"What are the tickets for, Lauren?" Jac hid a smirk at Vic's instant look of alarm.

"A Blue Rodeo concert at Randall Auditorium. My fiancé and I were supposed to be going, but he says he'd made prior arrangements for a football game with his friends." Lauren shook her head. "I'm sure I checked with him about the date before I bought the tickets, but he says I didn't. I can't get a refund, and I don't have anyone else to go with."

"I like Blue Rodeo," Jac fibbed. "Why don't I buy one of the tickets from you and keep you company?"

"Really? That would be great. But you don't have to buy the ticket—I'll just give it to you."

"No, I insist on paying for it. I wouldn't want to take advantage of you."

Victoria choked, and Jac patted her on the back. "Something go down the wrong way?"

Victoria sputtered into her napkin and glared at Jac.

Jac turned back to Lauren. "Why don't I call you at your office later in the week, and we can make arrangements?"

Lauren nodded, and Jac glanced at her watch. "I'm so sorry. I've really enjoyed our lunch, but I have to get back to work." Lauren raised her hand to signal the waiter, but Jac shook her head. "No, that's all right. I took the liberty of ordering a small treat, so please stay and enjoy it. It's your birthday after all. I hope you like chocolate."

Lauren beamed. "I love chocolate. It's a spiritual experience for me."

"Then I think you'll enjoy this. The chef only creates it for special occasions, but this seemed to warrant it." Extracting several bills from her wallet, Jac laid them on the table. "I think that should cover it. Enjoy your dessert, ladies. Vic, it was wonderful catching up with you. We mustn't leave it so long next time. And, Lauren, I'll talk to you in a few days, all right?"

"I'm looking forward to it, and thanks again for the roses. They are truly exquisite."

Jac left the table as the waiter arrived with dessert. She smiled at Lauren's rhapsodic exclamation. She knew the confection of chocolate mousse, white and dark Belgian chocolate shavings, and fresh strawberries was sure to delight.

That was actually a lot of fun. Lauren is good company. As Jac walked back to her office, she realized she was looking forward to the concert on Friday, but then reality set back in. *Unh-uh. Remember, this will be step two in the campaign, not a date.* She shivered as she left the sunshine and entered the lobby.

That did not go the way I hoped. Victoria paced at Lauren's side. She hadn't counted on the instant chemistry between Jac and Lauren, and tendrils of doubt began to grow in her uneasy mind.

"I don't think she was overpowering at all," Lauren said. "I like your friend. Maybe she left her hard shell at the office."

"Well, she was on her best behaviour." Victoria scowled at the sidewalk.

"And you didn't tell me she was drop-dead gorgeous. I'd kill for that hair. It's like molten rose gold, isn't it? And those blue eyes... Did you see every man's head swivel when she walked in? I can't believe she's single." Lauren laughed. "Good thing Phil wasn't with us, or I'd have had to blindfold him to keep him from drooling in his soup."

Fuck, fuck, fuck, fuck. "She does know how to make an entrance." Victoria had been certain Lauren would be immune to Jac's indisputable charisma, but she had watched her colleague closely as Jac wove her magic. She knew from experience how flattering it was to be in Jac's orbit. She'd seen Lauren blush when Jac turned the full force of her attention on her, and she'd heard Lauren's chuckles when her best friend gently teased.

With a frisson of misgiving, Vic summoned the mental image of Jac's arrival. She'd dressed in a royal blue suit to highlight her eyes. The tailored lines of the jacket clung to her lean body like a glove, and the skirt stopped just above her knees, which emphasized long shapely legs. A white silk blouse, small silver earrings, and a large silver pin on Jac's lapel completed the ensemble. Victoria hadn't needed to look around to know that virtually every male eye—and many of the female ones—in the restaurant were on Jac. She also hadn't missed Lauren's small intake of breath when she first saw Jac.

They'd almost reached the travel agency, and Victoria glumly noted that Lauren had yet to stop talking about Jac and the luncheon.

Damn. I'd better start planting suggestions to get Roger used to the idea of trying Sous-terre some night.

Chapter 4

THE DENSE CROWD EXITING THE auditorium carried Jac and Lauren along with it. Jac glanced over her shoulder, reached back, and grasped Lauren's hand to keep them together.

Lauren raised an eyebrow, but didn't try to extricate her fingers.

When they spilled onto the sidewalk, Jac tugged Lauren out of the throng and then dropped her hand. As she zipped up her black leather jacket against the brisk evening, Jac looked over the mass of people flowing around them. "It'll take forever for that parking lot to empty. I know a nice little café about half a block away. Can I interest you in a coffee while we wait?"

"That sounds wonderful. Let's do it."

Jac stepped aside and motioned Lauren to precede her up the short flight of stairs. She enjoyed the view as she watched the sway of Lauren's hips and the way the faded blue jeans hugged her ass. Suddenly, a rush of desire so strong it made her knees quake overwhelmed her. *Down, girl. Patience.*

She tripped over a stair, but Lauren whirled and caught her, steadying Jac until she regained her balance. "New feet?"

Jac chuckled. "Just breaking the darned things in. Thanks for the rescue." She drew in a deep breath of cool night air.

They exited on street level, where the auditorium fronted a popular avenue of bars, clubs, and restaurants. The usual Friday night crowds sauntered down the sidewalks in couples and groups.

Jac placed a hand lightly on Lauren's back, steering her around pedestrians to the door of the café, which she held open. "They make a Bavarian torte here that melts in your mouth."

"Oh, you think you have my number, do you?" Lauren smiled. "Okay, but you'll have to twist my arm."

"Consider your arm twisted. I know you'll enjoy it."

They were led to an empty table. The waiter set down plain white coffee mugs and held out two pots. "High octane or unleaded?"

"High octane for me. Lauren?"

"Decaf, please. Phil will kill me if I keep him awake tossing and turning."

"Two pieces of Bavarian torte too, please." When the waiter had departed, Jac studied Lauren. "So, tell me about the man who's captured your heart."

"Well, his name is Phillip Emerson. He works for his father's company, Emerson's Luxury Auto."

"Oh, I know that place. I lust after that midnight blue Boxster in the showroom every time I walk by."

"Phil isn't a salesman. I mean, he was when we first met, but now his dad's got him working in management. We met about a year ago when I moved from my parents' farm near Stettler. He came into the agency to book a holiday and kept coming back, even after all of the arrangements were finalized. He's really sweet. I didn't know anyone here, and he took me under his wing, introduced me to his friends, and showed me the city."

Jac observed closely. There was affection in Lauren's eyes as she spoke of her fiancé, but not passion. "Have you been engaged long?"

Lauren's gaze dropped, and she fiddled with the cup in front of her. "A few months. We're getting married next spring."

The waiter returned with dessert and set plates on the table.

"Is something troubling you?" Jac took a bite as she waited for an answer.

Lauren toyed with her torte, and then finally set down her fork with a sigh. "I feel kind of rushed, you know. I mean, we'd only known each other for four months when Phil proposed. We hadn't even...um, well, you know." She blushed.

"I take it you have, 'you know,' now?" Jac grinned as Lauren's flush deepened. "I'm sorry. That's none of my business. Forget I asked."

"Well, once we were engaged, Phil said it didn't make sense to keep two apartments, so I sublet mine and moved in with him. We're looking for a house now, but Phil can't seem to settle on one that suits him."

"Maybe you should look at building a new one."

Lauren perked up at Jac's casual suggestion. "I'd love to do that—choose all the colours and materials right from scratch. I really enjoy decorating. I guess I'm just a nester at heart." Her face fell. "I did ask Phil if we could build, but he says that contractors just rip you off and you never know what kind of quality you'll get. He says it's safer to buy a proven property."

"Shouldn't you have an equal say in this? After all, it's going to be home to both of you."

"You'd think so, wouldn't you?" Lauren's eyes flashed for an instant, then her shoulders slumped. "But his dad is financing the house, so I guess he feels he should have the final word. Sometimes it's just easier not to keep arguing, you know?"

"Not really."

Lauren looked at her wryly. "I doubt that many men argue too long with you. Maybe if I was a foot taller, they'd listen to me, too."

"Oh, I don't know. I'd pit a terrier against a Great Dane any day. I suspect that when you find something you want badly enough, you won't let anything stand in your way."

The mood lightened, and they finished their torte. Lauren cleaned up every last crumb, and Jac grinned. "Like another?"

Lauren's twinkling eyes peeked out from under her dark bangs. "Would you?"

"I don't think I have room, but please don't let that stop you."

Lauren's teeth worried at her lip.

With a smile, Jac signaled the waiter over and ordered.

"I think I like going out with you. Phil always warns me that I'm going to put on weight, but honestly, I think my metabolism must work overtime because I never gain an ounce."

"No, you certainly aren't carrying any extra pounds." Jac didn't leave her time to respond. "You know what you were saying about liking to decorate?"

Lauren shot her a quizzical glance.

"I sure could use some help with my loft, if you're interested. I've got nothing in there but bare white walls and hardwood floors. Even the furniture is all relics from my university days. For quite some time I've been thinking that I should do something to spruce the place up, but I never get around to it. Would you be interested in lending me a hand and giving me the benefit of your talents?"

"How do you know I have any talent?" Her tone was cheeky, but Lauren's eyes sparkled with interest.

"Gut feeling. Do you?"

"Yes, I think so. I helped my sisters with the home they share in Edmonton, and they loved it." Lauren leaned forward. "Are you serious? Do you really want my help with redecorating?"

"Trust me, there's no 're-' about it, but yes, I'd be deeply grateful."

"All right then. This could be a lot of fun. When do we start?"

"Whenever you're ready. And the sooner, the better."

Lauren fumbled in her purse and scanned the schedule on her phone. "How about this Monday after work?"

"Great. I'll even make you dinner as a thank you." *Yes! Step three, locked and loaded.*

"Can you cook?"

"You doubt me?"

"Forgive me, but you don't really strike me as the domestic type."

Jac clutched her chest. "I'm wounded to the core. I do actually make a mean stir-fry for the nights when I get tired of takeout, so I promise I won't poison you."

The waiter arrived with another piece of torte which Lauren took audible delight in eating.

"So, you said Phil went to the game tonight. Too bad, because he sure missed a great concert."

It was true. The concert had exceeded Jac's expectations. She was an old rocker and favoured classic bands such as The Stones and Alice Cooper. There was nothing she liked more than having sex to the sounds of Santana blasting from her multi-speaker sound system. But she had enjoyed the evening, though she wasn't sure if that was entirely due to the music or had more to do with the enthusiastic company. Lauren had grabbed Jac's arm in excitement every time the band began one of her favourite songs, and fortunately she had many favourites.

"Uh-huh. It was great, wasn't it? But I know Phil was happier going to the game with his buddies. You know how guys are."

"Not really."

Lauren tilted her head. "That's the second time you've said that. Do I take it you're between boyfriends at the moment?"

"I'm getting the feeling that Victoria didn't tell you everything about me."

Lauren's brow furrowed.

"I'm gay."

"Oh, um, no, I didn't know."

"I hope that's not a problem. I figured she'd told you." Actually, Jac had no idea whether Victoria would mention her orientation to Lauren.

Lauren shook her head. "No, not at all. I would never let something like that bother me."

"Good," Jac said. "Then I won't let your being straight bother me either."

Lauren stared for a moment and broke out laughing. She reached across the table and patted Jac's hand, then returned to her torte with relish.

When they'd finished a third cup of coffee, Lauren checked her watch. "I'm afraid I have to get home soon. Phil will be back from the game by now, and he'll be wondering where I am."

They settled the bill and returned to the nearly empty parking lot at the auditorium where Jac walked Lauren to her bright yellow VW. "That colour sure makes it easy to find your car."

"It's one of the reasons I got it." After unlocking her door, Lauren turned and smiled. "I had a great time tonight. Thank you."

"So did I. I'm looking forward to Monday. I'll see you then, right?"

"Right." Lauren slid into the driver's seat and waved.

Jac stepped away, hands thrust deep in her pockets, and watched Lauren drive off.

Once inside her black SUV, Jac started the engine and let it idle as she contemplated options. Lauren had ignited a longing within, and she was too restless to call it a night.

She briefly considered The Arc but dismissed the thought of another unsatisfying seduction. "Jesus, I should just go home." She leaned her head back against the seat rest and sighed. Though part of her longed to do just that, there would be no sleep until she assuaged the agitation that prickled her nerves like quills. *Sousterre. No strings, no complications. It'll do.*

Decision made, Jac headed beyond the city limits with her destination firmly in mind.

Several hours after she returned home from the concert, Lauren was still awake, lying on her side, with Phillip's arm wrapped around her. She stared at the wall, unable to sleep and chafing at the heavy limb that encircled her. She listened to his deep, even breathing until finally, unable to contain her disquiet, she slid out of his embrace and stood up.

Out in the living room, Lauren curled up in the recliner and gazed out the window at the apartment building across the courtyard. She mused idly about the lives going on behind the windows—most darkened, a few not.

Unbidden, an image drifted into her mind's eye— an angular face framed by waves of copper hair, and brilliant blue eyes that seemed to see right into her, but never through and beyond her, as Phil's often did.

When they were in the café, Jac's entire attention had been focused on her. She'd listened intently and remembered everything that was said. Her regard never drifted; she never interrupted; and even when Lauren took off on one of her flights of fancy, Jac had smiled and followed her lead.

I don't remember the last time I felt so...comfortable with someone outside the family. She and Jac had laughed and teased as if they'd known each other for years.

Lauren considered Jac's revelation about her sexuality and shrugged. It made no difference to her. It had been fun having a girls' night out again. She'd missed that since moving away from her hometown. Lauren had been adopted into Phil's circle almost immediately upon her arrival in the city, so she hadn't ever tried to make an independent group of friends. With the exception of Victoria, she really didn't know anyone who wasn't primarily Phillip's crony or a girlfriend of one of his cronies.

It might just be time to change that.

Chapter 5

THE APARTMENT DOOR OPENED, AND Lauren looked up. *Here goes.* With a deep breath, she tossed her hairbrush on the bureau and went out to greet Phil.

"Hey, babe." Phil slung his suit jacket over a nearby chair.

She kissed his cheek.

Phil loosened his tie with a groan. "God, what a day. You wouldn't believe the mess that idiot Carpenter caused." He peeled off his shirt and tie, tossed them aside, and scratched his chest. After a long stretch, he wrapped his arms around Lauren and nuzzled her. "It's good to be home. What are we having for dinner?"

Lauren placed her hands on his chest and gently pushed him away. "I'm afraid you're on your own tonight, hon. I'm going over to a friend's to give her a hand."

Phil frowned. "What friend?"

"I told you about her. The woman I went to the concert with on Friday—Jac Lanier. She asked me to help her redecorate her loft, and I put some ideas together over the weekend. I just have to see what the layout is like so we can make some decisions. I'm really looking forward to the project. It should be a lot of fun."

"Shit, I wanted to spend some time with you tonight." Phil gathered her back into his arms. "C'mon, babe, blow her off. Stay home with me." He pressed harder against her.

Lauren sighed and extricated herself again. "No, Phil. I made a commitment, and I'm going to keep it. I won't be out late. You and I can have time together later."

He turned his back, walked into the kitchen, and snagged a beer from the fridge.

She took her jacket from the closet and picked up her purse.

"Think I'll invite a few guys over to watch *Monday Night Football*. You don't mind, do you, babe?" There was a hint of challenge in Phil's voice.

Which means I'm coming home to a bunch of drunks. Phil's friends would be lounging in the living room, the air blue with smoke, empty bottles and pizza boxes littering the floor. In recent months, he'd been better about taming his old buddies' rowdy behaviour around her, but he obviously was in no mood to accommodate her tonight. "It's your home, too."

Lauren took the elevator to the underground parking, and pushed the unpleasantness out of her mind. *I can hardly wait to see Jac's place. I hope my ideas will work out the way I imagine.* She entered Jac's address into her GPS and turned the VW toward the river. After she crossed one of the bridges that would take her downtown, she turned onto a side street and then made an immediate hairpin turn onto a small service road that paralleled the riverbank and went under the bridge.

She saw nothing that resembled an apartment. "Okay, what's going on here? Did the GPS have a bit-burp?" Then she noticed an old stone structure on a rise just past the bridge, and the GPS announced her arrival. "Huh, I've crossed that bridge dozens of times and never even noticed this place."

Nestled in the shadow of the bridge that soared above it, the building appeared to be one of the city's originals. It wasn't large—just three floors high and about sixty feet across. Several narrow floor-to-ceiling windows were set in each level. The windows had an odd silvery sheen that complemented the stone construction, although it was apparent they were not part of the original design. In the centre of the flat slate roof, a rounded turret jutted upward. A small covered parking garage abutted the building on the north side, and the single-lane service road ran between the building and the river. Several guest spaces were available in the small gravelled lot next to the parking garage.

Intrigued, Lauren locked her car and strode toward the front door. She entered a small alcove and saw three mailboxes and three intercom buttons, the topmost of which was labeled "J. Lanier." She pressed the button.

"Hello?"

"Hi, Jac. It's Lauren."

"Hey, Lauren. C'mon up. I'm afraid there's no elevator, so you'll have to take the stairs to the top floor."

"Okay."

The buzzer sounded, and the lock was released. Lauren pushed through the door to the base of a steep flight of stairs that ran up the inner wall. She admired the care taken even in the stairwell. Rich muted paint colours, textured wall coverings, and thick, sound-deadening carpets combined with intricate wood detailing to give a subtle air of opulence. Porthole windows were set at regular intervals and illuminated the stairwell with natural light. She kept her hand on the carved, solid oak railing as she climbed past the second floor and emerged on the third-floor landing.

Jac was leaning against her open door with a wide grin. "Guess I forgot to mention it was a walk-up, eh?"

"Uh-huh. I think you may have overlooked that. Must be tough when you bring in the groceries."

Jac laughed and stepped aside, motioning Lauren to enter. "Why do you think I don't cook most nights?"

"Well, I wouldn't have thought it was because of the stairs."

Jac followed and took Lauren's jacket. "Oh, ye of little faith."

Lauren walked farther into the loft and caught her breath. "Oh my God, this is beautiful."

The design of the loft gave an overwhelming impression of space. The outer walls were stone and the interior ones plain white, as were the crown mouldings and wide baseboards. Shimmering hardwood floors caught the rays of the setting sun through tall, narrow, west-facing windows.

The entire lower floor was open living space with a small kitchen to the rear, a corner fieldstone fireplace, and an impressive home entertainment system. A short circular flight of stairs led off the kitchen to the open-sided upper level where Lauren assumed the bedroom and bath were located.

Lauren trailed a hand over the stone wall. "How do you get away without insulation in Calgary winters?"

"I don't. That's not the exterior stone. The contractor tore out the old interior drywall, added insulation next to the exterior stone wall, and then put in new stone to give the impression it's a single wall. It was one of the big selling points for me."

"I can see why. It's gorgeous." Lost in admiration, it took Lauren a few moments to notice that the furniture was indeed as dilapidated as Jac had indicated. "Your home is spectacular, but I'm sorry I can't say the same about your furniture."

"I did warn you. Come and see the view, and then I'll give you a tour of the rest of the place."

Lauren followed Jac to the windows. The Bow River flowed below them, edged by groves of mountain ash and poplar, their leaves already changing from green to orange and gold. Across the river was the city's trendiest shopping area, which was home to quirky shops, cafés, and a large outdoor market.

"Part of what I love about this place is being right by the river," Jac said. "I often go running down there, and on weekends, I usually finish up in the market. There's a great bakery there that makes croissants to die for."

"Doesn't the noise of the bridge traffic bother you?"

Jac shook her head. "No. Actually, the walls are so thick that they deaden most of the sound. Besides, putting up with some noise is a small price to pay for the privacy of this location. Our nearest neighbours are far enough away to give the illusion of isolation, even though we're right downtown. Come, let me show you the upstairs."

She led Lauren up the circular staircase. On the upper level, two-thirds of the space was open and the other third closed off. A waist-high, wrought iron banister encircled the area, and much of the lower floor was visible. A king-sized poster bed backed onto the stone, and a walk-in closet was partially open. An old mismatched dresser and bedside table, a couple of chairs and lamps, a wooden filing cabinet, and a large rolltop desk comprised the entirety of the furnishings. The tall windows rose to an open-beamed ceiling. The only oddity was a short ladder, leading to a trapdoor in the ceiling.

Lauren looked from the ladder to Jac.

Her eyes sparkled with childlike glee. "That's the best part of this place and why I had to have the top floor." Jac grabbed Lauren's hand and pulled her across to the base of the ladder.

Lauren waited while Jac climbed up and pushed open the trapdoor, lifted herself through the opening, and extended a hand back down. "Come on up. You have to see this."

Lauren hoisted herself through the trapdoor, aided by Jac. She looked around. A line of tall, narrow windows circled the tower, which was made of the same unfinished stone as the lower walls. Except for the obstruction caused by the bridge, there was a 360-degree view of the city. "Hey, we're in the turret."

"We are. Over a hundred and fifty years ago, this was the original fire station." Jac closed the trapdoor and unfolded a sling chair that was leaning against the wall. She gestured for Lauren to take a seat. "And this vantage point served as an observation and bell tower. The stables for the horses were just over there." She pointed in the direction from which Lauren had driven in. "And they used the river to fill the holding tanks. This building was in service for about eighty years, until the city outgrew it and they had to build bigger fire stations. It's gone through numerous incarnations since then, but when they turned it into condos a few years ago, I knew I had to live here."

"It's wonderful." Lauren was enthralled by the sight of dusk gathering over the city as rays of ebbing sunlight flashed off of office towers. "No wonder you love it. I would too." Jac sat on the floor beside her. "Hey, don't you have another chair?"

Jac shook her head and gazed out the windows. "I don't usually bring anyone up here. It's sort of my private retreat."

Lauren studied Jac's face, now deeply shadowed by the fading sun. She rested a hand on Jac's shoulder. "Thank you for sharing."

"My pleasure."

It felt so natural to be sitting there, watching the waning daylight with Jac. It was only when a hand closed over hers that Lauren realized it had gotten so dark she could barely make out Jac's features.

"I promised to feed you, remember?"

Reluctantly, Lauren shook off the spell under which she had fallen.

Jac folded the chair and put it back against the wall before pulling up the trapdoor.

Lauren peered into the darkness. "Can you see well enough to get down safely?"

"Absolutely. Trust me. I won't let you fall."

"All right." Lauren followed Jac back down to the upper level.

"Watch your step." Jac flipped on a lamp. "Well, that's pretty much it up here, except for the bathroom. You can take a look in there, if you want."

Keen to see every bit of Jac's home, Lauren opened the door to a large bathroom and immediately noticed the unusual size of the bathtub. "Wow."

Jac chuckled. "I know. It's bigger than the average bath. I love long soaks, and standard tubs just don't give me room to stretch out, so I custom-ordered this one."

Lauren glanced over her shoulder with a grin. "I can see that, but geez, you've got enough room in there for four people."

"Hmm, well, two anyway."

A shiver ran down Lauren's spine as an unbidden image of Jac lounging in the tub with another person—a female person—flashed into her mind's eye. She hastily backed out and ran into Jac.

"Whoa there, tiger." Jac laughed as she placed her hands on Lauren's shoulders. "You almost mowed me down."

Lauren waited until Jac turned to the stairs before she spun around and followed. She raised a hand to her heated cheek. *God, could I be more of a country bumpkin? I hope she didn't notice.*

Back in the kitchen, Jac began to pull things out of the fridge.

"Can I help?"

"Sure. You can start washing and slicing the vegetables while I get the meat ready. Based on your selections at your birthday lunch, I assume you're not a vegetarian."

"No, not a vegetarian. I'll eat pretty much anything. My mom never stood for fussiness at the dinner table." Lauren washed the vegetables, then stood beside Jac at the counter, each with her own cutting board. She paused halfway through dicing a carrot to stare at the deft way Jac's blade flashed in swift, precise strokes.

"Geez, you could work in a Japanese restaurant. Where did you learn to cut like that?"

Jac pushed the thin slices of beef into a bowl. "My mom was a sous-chef back before female head chefs were readily accepted. She studied in Paris. In fact, that's where she met my dad. Anyway, I loved to watch her in the kitchen, so when I was just a little girl, Mom put a knife into my hands, and I seemed to have an affinity for it." She laughed as she retrieved a bottle from the fridge, shook it, and poured some of the contents over the beef. "Not for much else in the culinary arts, though, and Mom soon banned me from doing anything but slicing and dicing."

Lauren was charmed by the image of a miniature Jac working beside her mother, industriously wielding a paring knife.

She continued with her own chore as Jac pulled a battered wok from a lower cupboard. After setting it aside, Jac washed her cutting board and knife and took half the vegetables from Lauren's stack.

"Thief."

"Slowpoke." Jac winked. They swiftly completed the preparations, and Jac delegated the preparation of the rice to Lauren while she began the stir-fry.

Once Lauren had cooked the rice and cleaned up, she settled onto one of the high stools beside the island and watched Jac deftly stir the meat before setting it aside and steaming the veggies. She inhaled the aroma of garlic, sesame oil, and an indefinable tang. "What's in that marinade?"

"Sorry, state secret. I can't tell you."

Lauren was thrown for a moment, until the corner of Jac's mouth lifted in a smile. "Sure, it is. Seriously, what's in it?"

"No, sorry, I can't tell you. This recipe was handed down to me by my mother on her deathbed with instructions to take it to my grave."

"No way."

"Yeah, you're right. My mom is alive and well, and running her own restaurant in Montreal." Jac ducked as Lauren tossed a peapod at her.

"Messy child. Why don't you quit harassing the chef and open the wine. You'll find a corkscrew in the right-hand drawer."

Lauren uncorked the bottle and slid two glasses out of the overhead holder. She filled one and set it beside Jac, then poured her own glass. "Anything else I can do?"

"No, it's just about ready." Within moments, Jac set two filled plates on the island and sat down opposite Lauren. Lifting her wine glass, she touched it to Lauren's. "Cheers."

"Cheers."

Jac took a swallow of her wine. "Mmm. That's good. Please eat while it's hot."

Lauren speared a forkful. "Oh, this is great. You *have* to give me the recipe."

"I don't know about that. I only have a couple of dishes I do well, and if I give you the recipe, it won't be special when I make it for you again."

Lauren halted mid-bite. A rush of pleasure swept through her. She'd never had a friend who wanted to keep something special to make for her.

"So did you come up with any ideas this weekend?"

"I did, but just general things since I didn't know what I was working with." Lauren grinned. "Acquiring new furniture will be close to the top of the list."

"Good. There's a spring in the couch that makes me feel like I've been on Torquemada's rack every time I fall asleep on it."

"Well, you have a perfectly lovely bed upstairs. You don't have to sleep on the couch. Actually, that's about the only thing that we don't need to replace. It looks in good shape. How's the mattress?"

"I haven't had any complaints so far."

Lauren choked on her wine.

Jac regarded her closely. "Are you okay?"

"Sure, no problem." Lauren coughed several times.

"I'm sorry. I didn't mean to strangle you."

"Quite all right, really." Lauren patted her chest. "It just went down the wrong way."

"Okay. Back to the matter at hand, I actually did buy a new mattress set when I moved in here, so we don't need to replace that."

"Good, I'll take that off the list, then." *And try to scrub my brain of that particular image.*

After Lauren had finished a second plate, Jac asked, "Do you have any room for dessert?"

"Always."

Jac laughed and collected the dishes before she retrieved a pint of ice cream from the freezer and two spoons. "Okay to share this way?"

"Ohhh, Häagen-Dazs. We can certainly share; however, I feel I should warn you, I'm pretty fast." Lauren ate a spoonful of the chocolate confection and returned for a second as Jac took her first bite.

"Remind me next time to get two pints."

After they finished the ice cream, Lauren pulled a small notebook from her purse. They spent an hour discussing colour and accessory options.

Finally, Jac stood and stretched. "Why don't we move to the couch? I know it's not the most comfortable thing in the world, but it beats these chairs."

"Only if you point out Torquemada's spring before I sit down."

"Just don't sit on the middle cushion and you'll be okay."

Lauren sank into the mottled mushroom-coloured couch at one end.

Jac activated the gas fireplace and settled on the opposite end.

"So, would you like me to give you a hand with the painting?" Lauren asked.

"You'd do that?"

"Sure. After all, if I'm to be the architect of this project, I want to make sure all aspects are done right. Besides, after we get the walls and trim painted, we can start with the good part—shopping for new furniture."

Jac groaned. "Shopping? Can't we just go online and order new stuff?"

"Where's the fun in that?" Lauren chuckled at the mournful expression on Jac's face. "We can get some things online, but I'm still taking you shopping for art pieces and accessories."

"I guess that wouldn't be too bad. Okay, so I'll pick up the paint and supplies, and we'll start on Saturday. Would that be all right?"

"Sure." Lauren scowled. *Oh, damn it, I forgot.*

"Is something wrong?"

"I think I'm supposed to be going to Phil's parents' place on Saturday."

"That's all right, I'll just start without you. Maybe you could drop by before or after to critique my work."

"Believe me, I'd rather be working here with you than going to the future in-laws. Phil's dad is all right, but his mother drives me crazy. Look, let me see what I can do, and I'll give you a call later in the week."

"Sure. Whatever works for you. I'm just grateful that you're taking time out of your busy schedule to lend me a hand. I love your ideas. I think your input will make this a home to really be proud of."

"It already is. We'll just be gilding the lily."

Jac shook her head. "This lily needs some heavy-duty gilding."

"Then I'm your woman." Lauren could already visualize the improvements, and she could hardly wait to get started. It took a moment before she realized that Jac had gone quiet. She reached across the space between them with her foot and nudged Jac's leg. "Hey, everything all right?"

"Absolutely. I've just...I'm really enjoying this evening. I'm so glad you and Vic let me crash your birthday luncheon."

"Me too. But I'm afraid I've monopolized your whole evening. I'd better go."

"Please don't go on my account. The night is young, and you're great company. Stay as long as you'd like."

"Thanks, Jac. I've had a wonderful time, too, but Phil was probably expecting me an hour ago, so I'd best go."

Jac rose to escort her to the door and held her jacket for her.

Lauren slid her arms into the sleeves. *I should get Jac to give Phil lessons on how to be a gentleman...gentlewoman?*

"Goodnight, Lauren. I can't remember the last time I had so much fun planning work. I hope you can make it back on Saturday."

"Me too. And thank you for a wonderful dinner."

When Lauren glanced back from the second-floor landing, Jac was watching her with an enigmatic expression. Lauren waved, and Jac returned her wave with a smile.

While driving home, Lauren pondered the evening. *A week ago we didn't even know each other, and yet I feel so comfortable with her. She has a real gift for putting people at ease. I don't know why Victoria said she has a hard shell. I sure haven't seen it.* Despite her inherent warmth, Lauren was shy with strangers, but her shyness had been nonexistent around Jac since the moment they'd met.

"I'm not going to dinner with Phil's folks. I'd far rather paint with Jac," she declared aloud. "Phil's going to have a fit, but it's all part of being a couple—working out conflicts and balancing our relationship needs with outside friends. It'll be good for us in the long run." *And it's better to set a pattern of not kowtowing to his mother right from the start.*

Jac stood at the window and watched the yellow VW drive away. When it was out of sight, her gaze drifted to the river. Its dark waters were lit only by the lights along the running path. It always calmed her to watch the endless flow, and tonight her mind desperately needed that peace. *What the hell happened?*

She hadn't intended to make a friend. It was irrelevant whether she liked Lauren or not; the only thing that counted was getting her into bed before the deadline. Yet, she had lost herself in the sheer pleasure of Lauren's company. *What in God's name is wrong with you?*

The river refused to work its soothing magic, and Jac turned away from the window.

Get your mind back on track. You seduce her; you fuck her. That's it. Game over—you win. She tried to focus on her goal, but the insidious warmth that Lauren's image evoked made it impossible.

Jac flung herself onto the couch. It was going well so far. She hadn't been oblivious to Lauren's hand resting on her shoulder in the turret, her blush when she'd backed into Jac, or the way Lauren had choked when she'd mentioned her bed. "I know when I'm affecting a woman. Lauren might not know it yet, but she is reacting to me."

Jac tried to concentrate on the moment of victory. She closed her eyes and pictured Lauren naked in her bed, arms open and legs spread to receive her, but instead of arousing her, the imagined victory was hollow. An image of Lauren's face, eyes filling with tears, seared across her mind's eye. Her eyes flew open. "Stop it! Maybe I'm doing a good thing here. Phil sounds like a dick. Maybe she'll realize it once she sleeps with me, and I'll have saved her from a lifetime of Phil-ness."

Jac suddenly realized that she was inhaling deeply. Puzzled, she focused. Her head rested on the pillow that

Lauren had leaned against; it was her scent that she was breathing in. With a deep groan, she seized the pillow from under her head and hurled it across the room.

"You've got five days to get yourself under control, you idiot. Now do it."

Chapter 6

"It's not like we were going to be the only guests," Lauren said. "Your parents invited half the city, so they're not even going to miss me. We'll have them over for dinner next Sunday, and they'll be fine."

Phil scowled. "What about me? What if I miss you? Jesus, lately it's like I don't even count. You go to a concert without me. You go traipsing off to see some woman who I don't even know and spend half the night there. What's Mom going to think when she finds out that you'd rather go help a stranger than be with your fiancé?"

Lauren's temper flared. "Twice. I've been away from you twice in the last week, so I hardly think you've been abandoned. And I asked you to come to the concert, but you had to go to the stupid football game with your friends instead."

"Is that what this is all about? You're pissed off because I ditched the concert? That is so goddamned petty."

Lauren took a deep breath and started to count to ten. She only got to three. "What this is about is that I made a new friend and you can't stand it. God forbid I'm not around twenty-four hours a day to dance attendance on you and your gang of juvenile slobs."

Phillip glared at her, spun and stomped out of the bedroom. He slammed the door behind him so hard that it bounced back and hit the wall.

Well, that went well. Lauren sighed. Phil would now expect her to seek him out with apologies and placating words as she always did after they fought. She grimaced. "Not this time. It's his problem, not mine." If she mollified him, it would mean acquiescing to his plans and going to his parents' party. *And that's not going to happen.*

Lauren stared at the vibrating door for long moments, then shook her head. She took a bag from the closet and packed a change of clothes for the evening, then picked up her keys and wallet and strode out of the apartment with barely a glance at Phil, who was glowering at the living room TV.

Lauren pulled into Jac's parking lot and turned off the car. "Okay, just let it go. It wasn't your first fight; it won't be your last. Focus."

Jac buzzed her into the building, and Lauren trudged up the stairs, bag in hand. She rounded the second-floor landing, stopped short, and burst into laughter.

Jac stood at attention at the top of the stairs, saluting with a large brush while her other hand held a paint can and long-handled roller. She wore a blue baseball cap on backward, grey fleece shorts, and a cropped black T-shirt; her feet were bare. She was also sporting the silliest grin Lauren had ever seen.

"What are you doing?" Lauren asked between fits of laughter as she climbed the rest of the way up.

"Reporting for duty, boss." Jac's eyes twinkled.

Lauren shook her head with a grin. "You are such a goof."

"Well, you did say you were the head of this project, so I thought it only proper to greet you with deference and respect." Jac followed her into the loft and closed the door.

"Uh-huh." Lauren surveyed the loft, and laughter bubbled anew. All the furniture had been pushed up against the stone wall, and drop cloths covered much of the remaining floor space.

"You know, if you'd gotten just one or two drop cloths, we could've moved them as we worked."

A crestfallen expression crossed Jac's face.

"It's okay," Lauren said. "This will work fine. It's just that you didn't need to spend all that money."

"No big deal." Jac set the can of paint down next to half a dozen others and a pile of painter's gear. "I've never done anything like this before, so I decided to err on the side of abundance."

"Well, you did that." Lauren surveyed the equipment wryly. "Guess I should've been more specific about our requirements. Remind me to never again send you to a hardware store alone." She picked up a small triangular foam piece. "What's this for?"

"Um, I think it's to do corners of windowsills. I got everything that I thought we might need."

Lauren smiled. Jac's zeal was engaging, if somewhat misguided. There were enough supplies to do three apartments, but it was nice to have an enthusiastic partner. "Okay, I'll just dump my stuff and we'll get started. Did you get all the walls washed?"

"Yes, ma'am. All washed and ready to go. And I taped off the nonpaintable areas, as per your instructions. You can throw your bag in the closet, or up in the bedroom if you want to keep it out of the way. Did you bring a change of clothes?"

"Definitely. I'm not going out to dinner in these." Lauren indicated the old sweats and T-shirt she was wearing. "You know, you don't have to—"

"Nonsense." Jac shook her head. "You're doing all this work for me; the very least I can do is feed you. Besides, I owe you, since you're missing dinner with your folks."

"Phil's folks." Lauren deposited her bag in the closet in the entryway. "And trust me, it's not like I mind."

Jac knelt to peel plastic off a paint tray. "Was Phil okay with you helping me out today instead of going to his family's place?"

Lauren winced. "I wouldn't exactly say he was okay with it, but he'll get over it."

Jac toyed with the tray. "I don't want to make trouble between the two of you."

"You didn't make any trouble. I'm where I want to be today, got it? No one makes me do anything I don't want to do."

Jac raised her head and met Lauren's gaze. "I'll remember that." She held out a roller and pan. "So, going to show me how it's done?"

They started at opposite ends of the same wall and worked steadily, chatting as they covered the white walls with a soft dove grey.

Jac carefully edged the lower moulding. "I was online last night, and I saw a couch and love seat that should meet with your approval. They're a blend of blue and grey, with a touch of maroon, and they look really comfortable."

"Sounds perfect." Lauren wiped at a spot of paint on her nose and only succeeded in smearing it. "I was thinking about your bedroom furniture, too. Your dresser and desk are old, but both are good solid wood, so I think we should refinish them rather than replace them. We could stain them mahogany to match your bed."

"Hey, you're supposed to be putting the paint on the wall, not your face." Jac set her roller down, cupped Lauren's face in one hand, and wiped away the smeared paint with the edge of her T-shirt.

Lauren glanced at Jac's top. "Thanks. You know, we do have rags. You're going to ruin your clothes."

With a grin, Jac shrugged and returned to her roller. "I've got so much paint on me already that one more spot won't matter. Besides, this shirt is going to be my badge of honour. If anyone ever doubts that I helped paint my own place, I'll just dig it out and wave it in their face."

"Maybe I should make you a certificate of achievement to signify your first successful foray into home decorating."

"If you do, I'll frame it and hang it over my desk." Jac poured more paint into her tray.

Lauren glanced up at the loft. "You don't have anything but thin air over your desk."

"I meant my desk at work. I'll give it pride of place, right beside my MBA. So where did you learn how to do all this stuff? Do you have a secret desire to be an interior decorator or a contractor?"

"I did once dream of being an interior decorator, but it actually comes from growing up in a large family where we were all expected to help out. Mom did most of the maintenance in the house while Dad worked the farm, and she never let anything go to waste. She could paint, spackle, roof, butcher a deer, can vegetables, sew clothes, refinish and upholster furniture. I think the only thing she didn't do was make our shoes, and I'm sure if she'd had more hours in the day, she'd have figured that out too."

Jac's eyebrows rose. "Wow, the original superwoman, eh?"

"I never thought of her that way, but yes, she's pretty incredible."

"Must be. She raised a pretty incredible kid."

"Um, thanks." Lauren took a moment to bask in the compliment. "And actually, she raised eight of us."

Jac's head snapped up. "Eight? God, she must have had stamina. I don't think I could handle one."

Bitter Fruit

"Oh, I dunno. Seems to me that you could handle just about anything you set your mind to. Anyway, Mom and Dad never set out to have so many. They didn't think they could have children, so they decided to adopt. Most of my brothers and sisters were older children that no one wanted for one reason or another. The two who came to us as babies, Zac and Sara, are special-needs kids. Mom and Dad just couldn't say no whenever Social Services came to them with a child who needed a home. Anyway, when Mom got pregnant with me, it was a complete surprise. Then she had my little sister a couple of years later, and finally said 'enough.'"

"Christmas around your place must be something else." Jac's tone was wistful.

"Is it ever. Even as adults, everyone goes home to Mom and Dad's for the holidays. It's a madhouse, but I wouldn't miss it." Lauren's shoulders slumped. "Though I might have to miss it occasionally now. It just about drove Phil crazy when I took him home weekend before last, and only half the family was there."

Jac raised an eyebrow.

"He's an only child, so he's not used to all the noise and commotion." *Though heaven knows he doesn't mind it when it's his friends raising the roof.*

Jac nodded.

"So, what about your family? Do you have siblings?"

"I do. I have an older brother who helps run Mom's restaurant. Leon is married, with a couple of kids, which thrills Mom to no end. And I have a younger brother, Marc. We're never sure where Marc is going to be from month to month, though he spent the whole summer in

Vancouver this year. He's got wanderlust, and will work at just about anything that'll put gas in his '65 Mustang and get him back on the road. I never know when he's going to pop up on my doorstep." Jac stopped painting, and gazed at the wall with a smile.

"Your favourite, right?"

Jac grinned. "That obvious, eh? Yeah, Marc is my buddy. We were best friends when we were kids and probably always will be. I know Leon gets mad at him because he won't settle down, but settling would kill Marc's spirit. I occasionally tease him about when he's going to grow up, but he says growing up is vastly overrated."

"What does your mom think?"

"Mom thinks the sun rises and sets on her baby boy's head. She tries not to show it, since Leon is the one who stuck with her and worked hard to help build the restaurant into a success. She doesn't want him thinking she's ungrateful or loves him any less, but Marc—well, Marc is a charmer, and has been since the day he was born."

They finished one wall and moved on to the next, again beginning at opposite ends.

"So does your mom know about you?"

"About me?" There was amusement in Jac's voice.

Lauren flushed. "Yes, well, you know—about you being gay and all. Does she have any problem with it?"

"Not really. I mean, I came out to her when I was twenty, and Mom's been pretty open-minded, for the most part." Jac bit her lip.

"But?"

Jac threw her a sheepish look. "But she doesn't like the way I run around. She figures I should find a nice girl and settle down, maybe give her more grandbabies."

"Hmm." Lauren concentrated on her strokes for a long moment. "And that doesn't appeal to you?" When Jac didn't answer, Lauren glanced at her. "Jac?"

Jac lowered her roller and half-turned to face her.

Lauren was surprised at the intensity in her gaze.

"It didn't used to. Now…now I don't always know. Sometimes I think it would be great to come home to the same woman, to go to sleep and wake up with her every day. To know she'd always be there for me, just like I'd always be there for her." Jac shrugged and resumed painting. "Hell, I'm just getting old, I guess."

Lauren considered her words. "No. It sounds to me like you just want what all of us want eventually—love, security, stability. It's not such a strange dream. I hope you get it. I hope you find that someone."

Jac took a deep breath. "Thank you."

Lauren focused on her roller's path. "Um, Jac? When you called to talk to Victoria on Wednesday—I mean, I wasn't trying to eavesdrop, but our desks are so close I couldn't help…"

Jac stopped and studied Lauren.

"I…well, I couldn't help overhearing, as I said, and…" *Jesus, I've only known her for a couple of weeks. I can't ask her this.* "Um, forget it. It was nothing."

Jac walked to her side. "Hey, it's okay. You can ask me anything."

Heat rose up Lauren's neck and she was unable to meet Jac's gaze. *Damn it. Why did I bring this up?*

"Lauren? Come on, talk to me." Jac touched her arm. "What's going on in that lovely head of yours?"

She took a deep breath. "Victoria said something on the phone about you being tired because you'd been out all night, and she teased you about being somewhere called sue-tair—at least I think that was the name. I'd never heard of the place, so I asked Phil that night. He just about swallowed his tongue and wouldn't tell me anything, except that he wasn't even sure if the place really existed, and if it did, I sure as hell didn't need to know about it. I tried Googling it, but nothing came up. So I was wondering…"

"What kind of a place would give Phil apoplexy?"

"Sort of." Lauren forced herself to look up. Jac wasn't glaring at her. In fact, her expression was hard to pin down. *Wistful? Perhaps. Or sad, maybe.*

Jac turned, scooped up one of the unused drop cloths, draped it over the old couch, and motioned Lauren to join her.

She set down her roller and took a seat facing Jac, who stared at the floor. She laid a hand on Jac's paint-spattered arm. "Please don't feel you have to answer. I had no right asking. I'd just never heard of the place, but it's none of my business."

Jac blew out a breath. "You haven't heard about it because it's a very, very private and very exclusive club. I doubt Phil has heard more than rumours. The only way to gain admittance is to belong, or go as a guest of a member."

"And you belong?"

"I belong." Jac shifted uneasily. "I guess—well, there's really no other way to put it: Sous-terre is a club for like-minded people who enjoy the more exotic aspects of sex."

Lauren blinked. *That's kind of what I thought after the way Phil reacted.* "Exotic?"

Jac squared her shoulders and met Lauren's gaze. "Domination and related activities."

A wave of sensual excitement washed through Lauren. *Wow.* "So, I guess you're into that kind of stuff?"

Jac leaned back with a wry smile. "You could say that."

"How did you—do you mind talking about this? Because it really is none of my business."

Jac shrugged. "It's all right. It's part of who I am. Ask whatever you'd like."

"I'm not really sure what to ask, but I am curious about how you got into such a…"

"Scene? The first time I went to Sous-terre, it was with a girlfriend who knew one of the owners. I didn't know what to expect, but when we got there, what we did appealed to me."

"So, you kept going because of your girlfriend?"

Jac shook her head. "I call her a girlfriend, but she was more like an extended one-night stand. We had one thing in common, and when that got old, we stopped seeing each other. I think she moved away a few years ago, but we'd long ago lost touch."

Lauren sat quietly, a dozen questions tumbling over in her mind. "What is it about the place, about what you do there that draws you back?"

"I suppose one of the main things is that everyone who goes there knows why they're there, so there's no hypocrisy or gamesmanship about hooking up with someone, whether for an hour or a night. There are ground rules—safe, consensual play, and absolute discretion about the club. You're never going to see Sous-terre on Facebook or any other social media. Among ourselves we call it 'Little Vegas.' You know—what happens there stays there, so it's a really secure place to let go. Nobody expects more than you're willing to give, and nobody gets their feelings hurt if you say no."

Lauren's brow furrowed. "I have to say, it doesn't really sound very…well, I guess, romantic, for lack of a better word."

"It's not supposed to be. We don't go there expecting to meet our life partners, though I actually do know of one couple who met there and are now married. We go there for one purpose—sexual recreation—and that's what we get."

"Is it legal?"

"It's just consenting adults getting together at a private club. The owners don't allow drugs or alcohol on the premises, so they don't need a liquor licence. In fact, if you go there drunk, you're not going to be admitted. The owners are very strict about that. It's outside city limits, so they're pretty much left alone. They're also well connected within the local power structure, and given some of the players I've seen there, I doubt the cops are going to raid it anytime soon."

"Is it just for women?"

"No, it's mixed. There are separate playrooms for men and women and straight couples, but there's a lot of wandering around between them, depending on what you're in the mood for."

"Doesn't it hurt?" *And is that the stupidest question I could ask?*

"Depends on what role I take, but yes, it certainly can. But it's the mental aspects comingled with the unrestricted sexuality of it that…well, that I find most stimulating."

Lauren was having trouble squaring her impression of Jac with this new information. "So you hurt others?"

"Sometimes, yes. You understand that anyone participating is doing so of their own free will, right? It's entirely consensual, and one of the reasons the owners vet potential members so thoroughly. They don't want someone getting hysterical over a bad experience and ruining it for everyone."

"I get that. I do. I guess… Okay, what if you're not at the club?"

Jac tilted her head. "You mean if I'm on a regular date, and we end up back at my place or hers?"

"Yes, exactly. Then do you…um…have sex normally?" *Jesus, she's going to think I'm some kind of voyeur…or fresh off the farm.* "Are you sure you're okay with me asking these things?"

Jac chuckled. "I am. As to 'normal' sex, what's normal? What you and Phil do together might be completely different than what goes on between the couple next door, right? As long as it's good for the people involved, what else matters?"

"You kind of dodged the question."

"I didn't mean to. Okay, say I'm at The Arc, I hook up with a lady, and we go home together. I'm never going to pressure her to do anything that makes her uncomfortable, but yes, if she seems inclined, I might suggest a few things out of her normal purview. If she's good with it, great. If not, I back off and let her set the pace. Does that answer your question?"

"Mmm."

Jac smiled gently. "Have I shocked you? I half-expected you to take off running."

Lauren feigned a glare. "I'm not a spring lamb, you know."

"Uh-huh."

She rolled her eyes. "I know you broke up with the first girlfriend who took you to Sous-terre, but what about other girlfriends? If you're dating someone, is she okay with you going there solo? Or do you expect her to go there with you?"

Jac looked away. "I don't exactly—I mean, it's been a long time since I—oh, hell." She turned and drew her knee up as she faced Lauren. "I'm not good at relationships. I haven't exactly 'gone steady' since my university days. I guess you could say that I play the field."

"Why? Because it's hard finding a woman who likes what you like—I mean, with the club and all?"

Jac shook her head. "No, that's not it. I've met a lot of women over the years who weren't averse to domination and other aspects of unconventional sex. I probably could've settled fairly happily with some of them, but I've never met the one with whom it wouldn't be 'settling,' the one who makes everything else in my life unimportant because she completely dominates my heart and mind."

"And body?" *Oh, for crying out loud. Open mouth, insert foot.* Lauren blushed at the images that sprang to mind.

"Not necessarily. Yes, I'd like to fall in love with a woman who's sexually adventurous, because frankly it's fun and exciting, and I can't imagine having nothing but vanilla sex for the rest of my life. But when it comes down to it, if I imagine that elusive woman, it's a much more domestic picture: kids, dogs, white picket fence. I hate to admit it, but exactly the life my mother's always nagging me to find. Don't you hate when your mother's right? Your mom is probably thrilled that you're settling down with a good man, and no doubt will soon be bringing your own babies to join in all the fun at the old homestead."

"I suppose."

Jac's eyebrows rose.

Lauren stood. "Hey, these walls aren't going to paint themselves. We'd better get back to work."

Jac looked at her sharply, but followed Lauren back to the roller pans.

Lauren tried to focus on the task at hand, but Jac's words rolled over and over in her mind. When Jac went upstairs for a few minutes, Lauren stopped painting and gazed out the windows. *She's not at all what I thought she'd be. Or maybe she is, but there's a lot more than first meets the eye. She's definitely not boring.*

Chapter 7

WHEN IT CAME TIME TO break for lunch, Jac produced a variety of elegant croissant sandwiches and set the array on the island, along with plates, napkins, and soft drinks. Lauren's eyes widened. "Wow, don't tell me you learned pastry baking from your mom, too."

Jac shook her head. "No. I ran down to the market early to pick these up. I figured I'd have to do better than last night's leftovers if I was going to work you all day."

I love how thoughtful she is. I could get used to being treated like this. The sandwiches melted in her mouth, and before she knew it, Lauren had eaten three and was eyeing a fourth.

Jac stifled a grin behind a napkin, and Lauren virtuously pushed temptation aside.

When they stopped again for a midafternoon break, Jac returned from the kitchen with two Cokes, another croissant, and a big smile. Without a word, she joined Lauren on the couch and handed her the plate.

"Oh no, I shouldn't."

Jac raised an eyebrow.

"Oh, all right. Twist my arm." Lauren bit into the sandwich.

Jac sipped her pop with a smug expression.

By 6:00 p.m., all the walls and the underside of the upper level had received two coats of paint. Lauren stood in the center of the living room admiring the evidence of their hard work.

"I think you were right about the colour," Jac said approvingly. "It's going to be really easy to live with for a long time."

"Uh-huh. And it blends beautifully with the stone wall. By the time we finish the baseboards and mouldings, get the new furniture in, and add a few accent pieces, you're going to have a real show home here."

Jac touched her arm. "Thank you. I can't believe all you've done for me. I really owe you."

"Believe me, I've had fun doing it. I love discovering the hidden beauty in things."

"Me too. I just didn't know it." There was an underlying intensity in Jac's words. Then she smiled. "Well, boss, I think we'd better get cleaned up and dressed for dinner. I made reservations at The Grotto for seven, and you've got more paint on yourself than on the wall. I can't even tell your freckles apart now."

"Hah. I do? You should see yourself—long, tall, and spotted."

Jac looked down at herself and laughed. "I guess we could both do with some washing up. Do you want the bathtub or the shower?"

Lauren's throat tightened. "Uh, doesn't matter—either one is fine."

Jac started stacking empty paint cans. "Why don't you go up and soak some of that paint off in the tub? I'll clean up here and then grab a shower. It will only take us about ten minutes to walk to the restaurant, so we have plenty of time."

Lauren took a deep breath. "Okay. I won't be long."

She retrieved her bag from the closet and went upstairs. Once she had the water running, she inspected the extensive collection of bath oils and salts on the tiled tub surround. *She wasn't kidding when she said she likes long soaks.*

She settled on one with a clean herbal scent that reminded her of Jac and poured a generous amount under the running water. After laying out fresh clothes, she stripped off her paint wear, stuffed it into the bag, and slid into the water. "Mmm, nice."

A few minutes later, Jac entered the bathroom, opened the door of the glassed-in shower, and turned on the taps to adjust the water temperature. She closed the door, stripped off her clothes, and tossed them in the laundry hamper.

"I think you forgot something." Jac pulled towels from a cupboard and crossed to the tub. "Is one enough, or do you need another for your hair?"

Lauren swallowed hard. "No, one's enough, thanks."

Jac nodded and returned to the shower.

What the hell is wrong with me? This is no different than sharing a bed and bath with Anjali. Lauren slid under the water for a long moment and resurfaced, brushing water from her eyes. She was no prude. Growing up in a house with eight kids, privacy had been nonexistent. But she'd never been so conscious of another's body. *Talk about physical perfection. She could be an artist's model.*

Lauren tried to avert her eyes to give Jac the privacy she didn't appear to require, but her disobedient gaze kept drifting to the glass enclosure. Soap ran in rivulets down Jac's long, lean body, chased by cascades of water that sparkled and danced over her form.

Her mind turned to their earlier conversation, and Lauren imagined Jac at play in Sous-terre. *Jesus!* Her heart pounded, and her hand strayed between her legs.

Unable to look away, Lauren's breath caught as Jac raised her arms to shampoo her hair, a movement that pulled her firm breasts up in sharp relief. *God, she's beautiful.*

Lauren gasped, hastily washed herself, and leapt out of the tub. She was dried off and dressed before Jac even finished her shower.

Downstairs again, Lauren sat on the couch and listened to Jac moving about overhead. *What the hell is going on? I've never reacted to anyone like that. For God's sake, you'd think I'd never seen another woman naked before.* She took several deep breaths. *Okay, it's probably just because we were talking about Sous-terre. No big deal.* But she couldn't stop the persistent mental comparison between Jac's smooth perfection of form and Phil's hairy, thickset body. *It's not Phil's fault. He just takes after his dad, and besides, I'm marrying him for the inner man, not the outer one. Still, I should probably encourage him to get off the couch more often, if just for the sake of his health.*

Lauren's thoughts screeched to a halt when Jac descended the stairs, and her breath caught all over again. Jac wore close-fitting black jeans, an emerald-green pullover with a white button-down shirt underneath, and black demi-boots.

Lauren stood and thrust her hands into her pockets. "You look nice."

"Thanks. You look good yourself. Are you ready to go?"

"I am." She followed Jac to the door and picked up her bag on the way. The evening air was cool, and Lauren was glad for her thick fisherman's knit sweater. She tossed her bag into her car and followed Jac to the spiral staircase that took them to the bridge level where they crossed over the river.

Jac chatted easily as they walked. "Have you ever been to The Grotto?"

"No, I don't think so." Lauren began to relax. "My tummy tells me I've been neglecting it far too long. Tell me about the restaurant."

"Well, the first thing you have to know is not to let appearances put you off. Mario's decorating taste is nowhere near as good as yours, but the atmosphere is relaxed and the food is fabulous."

Lauren glanced at Jac. "Okay. What's so bad about the decorating?"

"Oh no, that's all the warning I'm giving you. I really think you need to see it for yourself to get the full impact."

Jac steered Lauren down a lane one block away from the main market area and pointed at a covered entrance.

"That's The Grotto. The whole restaurant is actually below street level."

"Really?"

"Uh-huh." Jac led the way down a narrow flight of stairs.

At the bottom, Lauren stopped short and stared in amazement. The restaurant was styled to look like an underground cavern, complete with stalactites and a series of smaller "caves" that housed three or four tables each. The truly shocking element was the colour. Everything was painted terra-cotta—walls, floors, ceilings, and stalactites. Even the tables had salmon-coloured tablecloths set with white and terra-cotta dishes. The effect was almost overwhelming. *Oh, my God. It feels like I walked into a bottle of Pepto-Bismol.*

Jac whispered, "I told you."

Lauren tried to stifle her laughter, but when a man walked up to them looking like he had stepped right out of *Lady and the Tramp*, she had to bury her face against the back of Jac's shoulder to muffle her mirth.

"Good evening, Ms. Lanier. How are you today?" There was a strong hint of the mother country in the maître d's speech.

"Hello again, Mario. I'm fine, thank you. My friend and I have been looking forward to your lasagna all day."

Mario leaned forward with a conspiratorial air. "It is particularly good tonight. You will enjoy yourself." With a wink, he turned to lead them to their table.

Lauren followed Jac, biting her lip until they were seated in one of the smaller caves with their menus and Mario had departed. "You could've warned me."

"And missed that look on your face? No way. That was priceless. Mind you, I think I had the same look the first time I came here. Trust me though, Mario's lasagna will cause you to forget everything else."

"It's that good?"

"Sublime. They make everything from scratch, including the noodles."

Lauren closed her menu. "Then I guess I don't need to look at this. I'll go with your recommendation." When the main course arrived, Lauren took her first bite of the pasta, closed her eyes, and moaned with pleasure.

"Guess now I know what you sound like during *la petite mort*."

Lauren blushed and ducked her head.

"I'm sorry. You just sounded so orgasmic over there. It is great though, isn't it?"

"Is it ever." Lauren dove into her meal while Jac ate at a slower pace, keeping their wine glasses filled as they laughed and talked through dinner.

Lauren finally pushed her plate aside with a sigh.

"Any room for dessert?"

She shook her head. "I know you're not going to believe this, but I don't think there's an inch of space available."

"Are you sure? Mario makes an incredible homemade gelato, and it's not too filling."

Lauren rolled her eyes. "You're getting awfully good at twisting my arm. Could we share one?"

"Perfect." Jac summoned their waiter and ordered dessert and coffee.

When the gelato arrived, Lauren lingered over each mouthful. "Mmm, you were right again." She stopped Jac from filling her glass with the last of the wine. "I have to drive, remember?"

Jac shrugged. "You could always bunk down at my place."

Lauren was silent for a moment. It was an alluring idea. Phil wouldn't be in a pleasant mood, and she had no desire to end such a wonderful day with conflict.

Finally, she sighed. "No, I'd better go home, but thank you. Besides, you just want me there so you can put me to work at the crack of dawn tomorrow. You'd probably put a paint brush in my hand before I even woke up."

Jac laughed. "Caught me."

"Anyway, I don't think I want to sleep on that old couch of yours. I strongly suspect there are things living in there."

"Tch, what kind of a hostess do you take me for? I'd have shared my bed. It is a king-size, for heaven's sake. There's a ton of room."

"I have seen your bed. You have enough room for *ten* people."

"Hmm, now there's an interesting thought." Jac did her best Groucho Marx leer, then squawked when Lauren swatted her arm. "Hey, it was your idea."

"Uh-huh, I can see it now, people sliding around on your satin sheets, slithering out on the floor from every angle." Lauren had a sense she should stop before her mouth got her into trouble, but she was enjoying the banter too much.

"Satin? I'll have you know my sheets are flannel."

"No way. Flannel? You?"

Jac feigned a wounded expression. "Yes, flannel. Why not?"

"You just don't strike me as the flannel type, my friend. Satin or silk, yes, but flannel?"

Jac leaned forward. "But flannel feels *so* good on naked skin, don't you agree?"

Lauren hastily took a sip of her coffee and tried to banish the instant image of Jac sliding her nude body between flannel sheets. "Ah, we should probably be going, don't you think?"

"Sure." Jac sat back with an impudent grin and called for the check.

"Please let me pitch in," Lauren said. "I've had such a wonderful time, it's only fair."

"Oh no. This is all on me. I have to keep my unpaid employee happy."

"I thought I was the boss."

"Sometimes it's more fun to be the underling than the boss, but if you want to be boss, that's fine with me."

Lauren's eyes widened. "You are so bad."

"But in such a good way." Jac handed her credit card to the waiter.

Is she flirting with me? I think she's flirting with me. Lauren shivered. It wasn't an unpleasant thought. *Must be force of habit...or the wine. She probably flirts with Victoria, too.*

They left the restaurant and ambled over to the market, window-shopping and people watching. A busker on the street corner was playing a lively tune on guitar and mouth organ. They stopped to listen and tossed some coins into his case.

Someone stumbled into Lauren, knocking her off balance.

Jac grabbed Lauren's arm. "Hey! Are you okay?" She scowled at the middle-aged drunk who swayed unsteadily in front of them.

"I'm fine."

The man fixed a bleary gaze on Lauren and grinned widely. "Sorry, darlin'. Hey, wanna have a drink with me?"

"No, thank you." Lauren tried to turn away, but he stepped in front of her.

"Aw, c'mon. Don't be stuck-up." He glanced at Jac. "You can even bring your friend along. I don't mind. We can all have a good time together."

He lurched forward, and Lauren retreated from the stench of his breath.

Jac stepped between them. "The lady said no. I suggest you take her seriously and move along…now."

Lauren's eyes widened at the icy words. She laid a hand on Jac's back. Her muscles were taut, and her hands had curled into fists.

The drunk flinched and turned aside. "Jesus, I was just offering a friendly drink. You don't have to make such a big deal about it, bitch." He stumbled away, still muttering.

Lauren exhaled as Jac turned to her.

"Are you all right?"

"Am I all right?" Lauren impulsively hugged Jac. "You were the one in the line of fire. Thank you."

Jac returned the hug. "You're welcome, but he was all talk. Really nothing to worry about."

Nothing to worry about with you around, that's for sure. Lauren linked arms with Jac. "I think the effects of the wine have dissipated some. I should probably get going."

Jac nodded and turned their steps in the direction of the bridge. Both were quiet on the walk back, but it was the comfortable peace of friends who know they don't have to fill up all the silences.

It's so easy to be with her. Lauren kept her arm tucked in Jac's until they reached the top of the spiral staircase. They descended to the river's edge and followed the path back to her car. *I wish this night didn't have to end.* When they reached the VW, Lauren turned to Jac. "Thank you. I had a wonderful time, despite the drunk. In fact, the whole day was a lot of fun."

"I'm glad, but it's me who should be thanking you. You worked hard, and I appreciate your help. I never knew that painting could be that much fun, though I think that had more to do with the company." Leaning forward, she brushed a kiss against Lauren's cheek. "Good night. See you tomorrow."

Lauren watched Jac walk up the firehouse steps. She touched her cheek as she got into her car, but she didn't start the engine until she saw the lights come on in the loft.

Chapter 8

Lauren looked up from her desk as Victoria entered the agency, coffee in one hand and umbrella in the other. "Good morning. Lovely day, isn't it?"

Victoria shook the drops off her umbrella. "Lovely? It's Monday and pouring rain. What exactly is so lovely about it?"

Dunno. It just feels like a lovely day, rain and all. "Did someone get up on the wrong side of the bed this morning?"

"There was no right side of the bed this morning." Victoria hung her coat up and took a seat at her desk. "You know, Roger was only gone for four days last week, but in that brief span of blissful silence, I totally forgot how badly he snores. I ended up having to stuff my ears with tissues about two o'clock in the morning just so I could fall asleep. I'm seriously considering making our guest room into my bedroom, to prevent myself from ending up permanently sleep deprived."

"I know what you mean. Sometimes Phil is so loud that I take refuge on the living room couch. I guess I'd better make sure we have enough bedrooms in our new place so I can escape now and then, too."

Victoria uncapped her large coffee and took a deep swallow. "Mmm, that's better. I might survive now. So did you and Phil make any progress on house hunting this weekend?"

"Actually, I spent most of the weekend working with Jac, so Phil and I didn't tour any houses."

Victoria choked and set down her coffee. "With Jac? What were you two doing?"

"Painting, mostly. We did all the walls, mouldings, and trim at her place. We ordered a new couch and love seat, and even stripped her dresser and bedside table. We ran out of time last night before we got to her desk, but she's supposed to work on that this week. You should see her loft. It took us all weekend, but her place is looking fabulous. By the time we're done, they could feature it as one of Calgary's finest in *City Magazine*." Lauren frowned. "Are you okay? You look kind of pale."

"I'm fine. I just...uh...didn't know you two were working together. I haven't talked to Jac since your birthday luncheon."

"Did I remember to thank you for that? If you hadn't introduced us, I'd never have met her, and we're having such a blast. She took me to the funkiest restaurant I've ever seen on Saturday night. I couldn't stop laughing at the décor, but the food was fabulous." Lauren studied Victoria. "Are you sure you're not coming down with something? Maybe you should take the day off and catch up on some sleep. I can cover your clients."

"No, no, I'm good. Just a little tired." Victoria swiveled the chair around to face her computer. "Excuse me. I need to catch up on e-mails."

Jac read Vic's e-mail again. Her friend was clearly upset, and it should've elated her. *She's just pissed that I'm winning.* But there was no joy in the knowledge, and she was far from jubilant.

She leaned back in her chair and gazed out the window. Despite all the hard work, the weekend had been fun, at least until Lauren left. They'd gotten a little giddy on fumes from the paint stripper they'd used on the dresser and bedside table and ended up rolling on the floor. She couldn't remember what they were laughing about, but it had felt good. It felt…right.

Before Lauren had had to leave, she'd given Jac detailed instructions on how to strip the desk, but the task had turned into a real chore. *It was no fun without her.*

Jac consulted her calendar, wondering if Lauren would like to have lunch with her this week. "Maybe I'll surprise her."

"Ms. Lanier? Your nine thirty is here."

Jac looked up and nodded. "Thanks, Becca. You can show him in."

She glanced at Victoria's e-mail again, then logged off. There was no point. She didn't feel like gloating, and Vic was going to be upset no matter what she said.

Jac carried the covered Styrofoam trays carefully as she walked down the sidewalk to the Trevor Travel Agency. A man exiting the agency held the door open for her, and she nodded her thanks as she slipped by him. The office, decorated with alluring posters of exotic locations, held six desks—four of which were occupied by agents on phones or at their computers.

She crossed to Lauren's desk and took one of the client chairs. "Hi."

Lauren grinned. "Hey, you. I didn't know you were dropping in today. If you're looking for Victoria, she's not in right now."

Jac slid one of the packages across the desk. "I know. It's the third Thursday of the month."

"What's this?" Lauren opened the tray, which released a burst of steam and piquant aromas. "Oh, wow, this looks great. Honestly, Jac, you're going to spoil me."

Jac shrugged. "It's only Thai takeout. Compared to all the work you did on my place last weekend, it's a small reward. I just thought it might be a more appealing lunch than a sandwich. Here, use these." She handed over a small plastic bag, and then opened her own lunch.

Lauren unwrapped the chopsticks and dug in enthusiastically.

Jac smiled. She'd had a hunch Lauren would like Thai, but then, she suspected Lauren had never met an ethnic cuisine she didn't like. Jac had rarely seen anyone who so enjoyed their food. She took up a forkful of spicy noodles.

"So, what did you mean about it being the third Thursday?"

"You mean you've worked with Vic a whole year now, and you've never noticed that she's always gone at noon on the third Thursday of the month?"

Lauren's chopsticks halted halfway to her mouth. "You know, I never noticed, but you're right. Where does she go?"

"She has a standing appointment with Ronaldo to have her hair done." Jac fanned her mouth. "Do you have water around here? I think I just burnt my tonsils."

Lauren laughed and pushed back her chair. She went into the back room and returned with two Cokes. Jac snapped open one can and poured the cold liquid down her seared throat with a sigh of relief. Lauren blithely returned to the spicy food without any sign of discomfort.

"Don't you find it the least bit hot?"

Lauren shook her head. "No, not at all."

Jac raised an eyebrow.

"Cast-iron stomach. It helps if you're not really picky when you're competing with nine people at the dinner table. I learned early to dig into whatever was closest and not worry about what it was."

"Makes sense, I guess." Jac gingerly picked through her meal, looking for the least potent part. "You didn't return my call last night. I just wanted to let you know that the furniture we ordered is going to be delivered on Saturday."

Lauren stopped eating and studied her. "You called last night?"

"Yes, about six thirty."

Lauren scowled. "I'm sorry. I didn't know you called. I was out grocery shopping, and I must have missed Phil's note when I got home."

Jac wasn't surprised. When Phil had answered the phone and she'd identified herself, he'd barely been short of rude. When Lauren hadn't called back, Jac suspected that her message hadn't been passed on. "No big deal. I just thought since you were instrumental in the shopping, you might want to see what you spent all my money on."

Lauren stabbed viciously at another shrimp, then took a deep breath and leaned back. "I do. Besides, we have to stain your bedroom furniture. We can do that while we wait for the deliverymen." Her sunny nature reasserting itself, Lauren waved a chopstick at Jac. "Did you finish stripping the desk?"

"Yes, boss, I finished it last night. What a job though. I can't believe how many nooks and crannies there are in my old roll top." Jac winked. "Fortunately, I'm very, very experienced with nooks and crannies."

Lauren started to choke, and Jac scrambled around the desk to pound her back. She grabbed her Coke and took a swallow, coughing several times as she waved Jac off.

The middle-aged woman at the next desk looked up in concern. "Are you all right?"

"Fine, Irene. Something went down the wrong way." Lauren glared at Jac, who had returned to her chair. "I can *not* believe you said that. You really are incorrigible. You could've killed me there."

"I know how to do the Heimlich."

"Do you really?"

"Um, well... I'm pretty sure I could learn it fast if I had to."

Lauren rolled her eyes. "Oh great. Remind me never to put my life in your hands."

You could put your life in my hands. Jac stared at her food tray and focused on slowing her racing heart.

"If we're going to do the staining on Saturday, why don't we hit the art galleries on Sunday? I've done a little research online, and I know exactly where to go first." Lauren snapped her fingers a couple of times. "Earth to Jac. Are you there?"

"Um, yeah, great. That sounds like a good plan." Jac shivered and pushed her lunch aside to toy with her Coke.

"Hey, I've got an idea. Why don't you come over to my place for dinner after we finish shopping? I already have a big dinner planned because the in-laws are coming over, and I'd love for you to meet Phil."

That caught Jac's attention. *Somehow I don't think Phil wants to meet me.* "I'd love to come, and thank you."

"Great." Lauren's grin faded. "I should warn you in advance though—Phil's mom can be a pain in the ass at times. Don't let her get to you, okay?"

"I'll be on my best behaviour, I promise."

"I'm not worried about you, but she can be as abrasive as sandpaper and I don't want her to get under your skin."

"Don't worry. I've got a pretty hard shell."

"That's what Victoria told me once, but I think you're both wrong." Lauren smiled warmly. "You're about as far from Yertle as they get, so don't think you can pull the wool over my eyes."

A knot tightened in Jac's chest.

"Anyway, as I was saying, Phil's dad is a good guy—you'll like him—and I really want you and Phil to get along, too."

"I'm sure we'll bond splendidly." *Judging by our little conversation last night, he'd sooner welcome a rattler into his home.*

They finished their lunch, and Lauren took the empty cartons to the back. When she returned, she walked Jac to the front door.

"Thank you. One of these days I'll return the favour and show up at your office with lunch. Or better still, I'll take you out somewhere."

"That sounds nice, but not for Thai, okay?"

"Wuss." Lauren held the door open. "All right, bland it is. And here I thought you'd be a woman of the world."

"I am. I'm just partial to keeping my taste buds nonblistered."

"So why would you buy Thai in the first place, then?"

"I thought you might like it."

There was silence. Lauren regarded her, eyes gleaming.

"See you Saturday." Jac turned away.

"Saturday. Definitely."

As she walked the few blocks back to the bank, Jac considered their final exchange. She had consciously selected a Thai lunch because she was sure Lauren would enjoy it. *Makes sense. I mean, I want her to like me, right? I'm certainly not going to win the challenge if she hates me.* But the rationalization felt hollow, and she slowed to a halt.

Damn it, when did this seduction become a courtship? People flowed around her as she considered the implications. *What now?*

Jac picked up her pace, her stomach roiling. *Lose to Vic? No way. Never going to happen.* But as she entered the bank and nodded at the doorman, Lauren's shining eyes and sweet smile filled her mind. *I'm in trouble. Really, really in trouble.*

Chapter 9

JAC FLEXED HER LEGS AND wriggled in her seat. "Volkswagens are definitely not made for tall people."

Lauren smiled. "Sorry, when I bought this car, I didn't know I was going to have a giantess for a friend."

"That's okay. I didn't know I'd be hanging with a midget."

Lauren shot her a mock scowl. "Who're you calling a midget?"

"Hey, if the shoe fits—the teeny, tiny, wee little shoe…"

Lauren smacked her shoulder, and Jac broke into a laugh. It had been such a good day. She continued to squirm in the restricted space, but smiled as she looked out the window. Lauren had dragged her all over the city, which normally would have driven Jac crazy, but she'd genuinely enjoyed their shopping trip. *And now I get to meet Phil and his dragon mother.*

Her smile faded. Part of her anticipated the confrontation, but she'd decided to take the high road, doubting that Phil would do likewise. Lauren hadn't said anything outright, but reading between the lines, it was clear he wasn't thrilled with his fiancée's new friend and all the time they'd been spending together. *This could be an interesting evening...in an old Chinese fortune kind of way.*

"There's home." Lauren nodded at a pair of apartment blocks ahead of them.

Jac surveyed the buildings. Generically constructed, there was little of interest about them. Diplomatically, she withheld comment as Lauren drove into the underground garage and parked. *My place suits Lauren far better, but I'll keep an open mind; maybe it's better inside.*

They went up the elevator, and Jac followed Lauren into the apartment. She looked around, surprised at how little of Lauren's stamp was on the insipid interior.

Almost as if reading her thoughts, Lauren shot her an abashed look. "Phil doesn't really like change."

Jac whispered, "Then Phil doesn't know what he's missing."

A burly man strutted up to them and gathered Lauren in his arms. He kissed her possessively, ignoring her quiet protestation.

Jesus, why don't you piss on her while you're at it? Talk about marking your territory. Jac kept the distaste off her face, maintaining a look of mild interest.

When Phil finally released Lauren, she was blushing as she turned and tugged Jac forward. "Jac, this is my...this is Phillip Emerson. Phil, this is my friend, Jac Lanier."

Jac was amused to see that she topped his height by at least four inches. She gave the scowling man a big smile and held out her hand. "I've heard so much about you. It's nice to finally meet you."

That wasn't the truth. Lauren talked a lot about her family, but very little about her fiancé.

Phil shook her hand. "Likewise."

He turned to Lauren. "Mom called. They'll be here in about an hour." Without a word or a backward glance, he returned to the living room where an NFL game was blaring on the television.

Lauren glanced at Jac. "Why don't I take your jacket, and then maybe you can give me a hand in the kitchen?"

"Sounds good." Jac handed over her leather bomber.

Lauren's shoulders were stiff with tension, and Jac regretted her part in creating the stress. "Something smells fabulous. How can that be when we were out shopping all day?"

"I put a roast on timer and made dessert before I picked you up."

"Ah, you are your mother's daughter after all, you magical multitasker, you."

Lauren smiled and her shoulders relaxed. "And you're just a sweet-talker. Are you sure your mother didn't meet your dad in Ireland instead of France? That red hair had to come from somewhere."

"Who knows? Maybe there was a leprechaun hiding under the honeymoon pillows." Jac winked and was rewarded with a laugh.

"Must've been the tallest leprechaun in the world, then."

"Phsst. Even leprechauns look tall when you're looking at the world from all the way down there."

Lauren giggled and bumped Jac with her hip.

Jac feigned being knocked off balance.

"Goof." Lauren pulled a potato peeler from a drawer and handed it to Jac. "You do know how to use one of these, right?"

Jac pursed her lips and turned the peeler over in her hands. "I guess I can figure it out. I use the sharp side, right? Bring on the spuds, madam."

Lauren dumped several potatoes into one side of the double sink and began to clean lettuce and vegetables on the other side. "I really like the purchases you made today. That sculpture is going to be the focal point of your loft."

"I know. I fell in love with it as soon as I saw it." The black marble torso of a nude woman, her head thrown back and face carved in an expression of ecstasy, had lines that flowed so naturally it took Jac's breath away. "Even if you'd let me pay full price, it would've been worth it."

"Full price—are you crazy? They were asking way over market value for it. You can't just pay sticker price without at least asking for a discount."

The two hundred dollars Lauren had talked them down by was pocket change to Jac, but she'd enjoyed watching her friend haggle. "Well, thanks to you, we got one."

"Yeah, I was satisfied, particularly when he gave me a discount on the tapestry too. It's going to look fabulous over your bed. I'm just sorry we couldn't take it right away."

Jac shrugged. "It's not a problem. After all, we'd be ticked if someone else took the one we'd already put a deposit on, but he said he'd have another for us in a couple of weeks. I don't mind waiting. Thanks for taking charge of that, by the way." Lauren had given the owner her numbers, with firm instructions to call the moment it arrived.

"You're welcome. If I don't hear from him within the two weeks, I may be able to negotiate an even better price."

Jac didn't bother to tell Lauren that the cost of all the art and accessories combined barely put a dimple in her savings. "If you can, great, but please don't worry about it. It's a fair price, and I don't want to skin the artisan. So, where do you think we should put the statue?"

"I'd like to see it in your living room...unless you'd rather have it in the bedroom."

"Are you kidding? I'd get an inferiority complex looking at it when I got dressed every day."

Lauren snorted. "Sure you would. You could've modelled for that thing yourself."

"So could you."

"Dream on."

Jac stopped peeling and turned to face Lauren with a serious expression. "I'm not kidding." *Vic was only half right—your beauty isn't just inside.* "I'd love to see what that artist could do with you as a model."

Lauren raised an eyebrow, then shook her head. "Thanks. You're a little crazy, but I appreciate it."

She shook the water droplets off the lettuce and began to tear it into a bowl. "So anyway, I thought what we'd do is get a white marble pedestal to put the statue on for contrast. I want to research art lighting, but I think we can use recessed lights to illuminate it softly at night. It'll be gorgeous."

"It will." *And I wish I could convince you that you are, too.* Jac grimaced. *Doesn't Phil ever tell you that? The man's a fool.*

They were setting the dining room table together when a sharp knock sounded at the door.

"Phil, would you let your parents in?"

Grumbling under his breath, Phil tore himself away from the game and went to the door.

Lauren sighed.

They quickly finished with the table, and Lauren went to greet her in-laws as Jac hung back and observed with interest. Lauren and her future mother-in-law greeted each other stiffly. Mrs. Emerson was a thin woman of medium height. Her rigid posture, lacquered platinum hair, and drawn features created an indelible impression of brittleness. Mr. Emerson was a burly, balding man who resembled his son but without the sullenness that marred Phil's features. After he and his wife handed over their coats, he strode over to Jac and offered his hand with a smile.

"I don't know if you remember me, Ms. Lanier. We met last year at a Chamber of Commerce luncheon. I sure remember you. Your presentation on commercial pitfalls for mid-sized companies was brilliant. Not to mention that you were the best-looking banker I'd ever seen."

Jac did remember him. He had cornered her after the luncheon with a multitude of earnest questions until her VP had intervened. "Of course—Frank Emerson. It was a pleasure talking with you on that occasion. As I recall, you brought up some interesting points on competitiveness."

Frank beamed. His wife cleared her throat ostentatiously behind him, and he started. "Oh, Ms. Lanier, this is my wife, Phyllis. Phyl, this is Ms. Lanier."

Jac extended a hand. "Please, call me Jac. It's nice to meet you, Mrs. Emerson."

The woman took the proffered hand and shook it limply, unable or unwilling to conceal her distaste. *Huh, wonder what her problem is?* Still, Jac nodded politely, ignoring Mrs. Emerson's overt antagonism. Lauren frowned, but Jac met her gaze with a subtle wink and garnered a small smile in return.

Frank monopolized Jac with talk of business, but when she noticed that neither Phil nor his mother made any attempt to assist Lauren, she excused herself and went to help.

"I hope you like roast beef. It looks like low and slow did the trick."

Jac nodded. "It certainly smells fabulous."

Lauren bustled about filling serving bowls, which Jac transported to the table. When she returned, Lauren was whipping the potatoes. She pointed at the roast standing on the carving board. "I've seen the way you handle a knife. Feel like carving for me?"

Jac pulled a large knife from the butcher block on the counter. "Sure. Do you like your slices thick or thin?"

"Here, I'll do that." Phil shouldered into the kitchen between them to stand in front of the roast.

Wordlessly, Jac turned the knife and extended it handle first. "Anything else I can do, Lauren?"

There were points of colour on Lauren's cheeks and anger in her eyes as she held out the bowl of potatoes. Jac exited the kitchen to put the potatoes on the table, but overheard Lauren's whispered question. "What is the matter with you? That was rude."

"Carving's a man's job. It wouldn't be right to ask your guest to do my job."

"Funny, that never stopped you before."

Jac's eyes widened. *Oh boy. I wouldn't want to be in his shoes tonight.*

She set the bowl on the table and joined the Emersons. Frank turned to greet her, but Phyllis shot her a sour look. "Excuse me. I'll just freshen up before dinner." She stalked off.

Frank gave Jac a forced smile. "So, how did you and our little Lauren meet?"

"Lauren works with my old friend, Victoria, at the travel agency. Vic took Lauren out for a birthday luncheon, and I first met her at the restaurant."

Lauren emerged from the kitchen. "Dinner's ready. Everyone come to the table."

Phyllis took the head of the table. Frank sat beside Jac and across from Lauren, while Phil slumped beside his fiancée. Lauren's posture was rigid, and she had a white-knuckled grip on her fork.

Okay, I need to lighten things up here. Jac engaged Frank in a lively discussion about the annual Christmas charity show sponsored by his company. "So you're thinking of re-directing your funds this year?"

Frank nodded. "We've been sponsoring the Mustard Seed for almost two decades now, and it's a worthy institution, but some of the board would like to spread the wealth around, if you know what I mean."

"What do you think, Lauren?" Jac asked. "Where would you direct the funds?"

"The women's shelter. The Mustard Seed does wonderful work, but I think the women's shelter gets overlooked too easily."

Jac tilted her head "Why is that?"

"Because they have to keep a low profile to protect the women and children who take refuge there."

"Good point. I think—"

"I think it's a waste of money."

All heads swiveled to Phyllis.

"Why is that, Mrs. Emerson?" *And doesn't that stick up your ass hurt?*

Phyllis sniffed. "Emerson Luxury Auto is a business, not a charity. Frank spends entirely too much time every fall organizing that foolish show. What kind of example to Phil is it to neglect business for months on end?"

Lauren levelled a cool gaze at Phyllis. "I'd say a very good one. I think we all have a duty to do what we can for those less fortunate."

Jac stifled a grin. *Atta girl. You tell her.*

"Nonsense. People who draw on such services simply have to pull up their socks. A little hard work goes a long way."

Yeah, I'll just bet you know all about hard work. It must be exhausting spending your husband's money. Jac could practically see the fire in Lauren's eyes, but she held her tongue.

"On a much more pleasant topic, I believe I've found the perfect house for you two." Phyllis glanced at Jac. "Phil and Lauren have been searching for just the right home. It has to be in a good neighbourhood of course, and have enough room for the children."

"Well, when they find it, I can certainly vouch for Lauren's talents in decorating it."

Phyllis waved her hand dismissively. "Don't be silly. That's what professionals are for. Lauren, the Carltons just put their house up for sale. It's perfect for you two, and I've made an appointment with the realtor to look at it Wednesday after work."

Lauren blanched.

Jac regarded her closely. *What's wrong with the Carlton house? She looks like she saw a ghost.*

Lauren was virtually wordless through the rest of the meal until Phyllis brought up the following weekend.

"Phil, dear, the Marquettes have changed the time next Saturday. We're to be there at three, not four."

Lauren's head snapped up and she looked at Phil. "Next Saturday? What's going on next Saturday?"

"I told you. We always go to the Marquettes for their fall fling."

"No, you didn't tell me. I asked you weeks ago if we could go to the farm for an early Thanksgiving, and you agreed."

"Was that next weekend?" Phil shrugged. "No can do, babe. The Marquettes' party is the unofficial start of the fall social season. Everyone goes."

"Not me. Anjali, Courtney, and Adam are coming home, and it's the first time we've all been together since spring. I won't miss it."

Phil glanced at his mother, whose gaze was boring into her son. "We'll talk about it later, okay?"

By the time dinner ended, Jac wanted nothing more than to leave. She helped Lauren clear the table and stack dishes in the kitchen. "I think I should get going. I'm pretty tired from all we've done this weekend, and tomorrow is a workday."

Lauren stared at the floor. "I don't blame you."

"Hey." Jac placed a hand on her shoulder. "Are you all right? I'll stay if you want me to."

Lauren gave a short, bitter laugh. "Now I know you're my friend."

"There was never any doubt."

Lauren beamed, but then her smile faded. "Wait a minute, how are you going to get home? I drove today, remember?"

"Don't worry. I noticed a cab stand at the hotel down the street. I'll get one there." When Lauren tried to protest, Jac placed a finger over her lips. "You can't abandon your guests."

"Can't I?" But her protest was half-hearted. "C'mon. I'll walk you to the elevator."

Jac bade the other guests goodnight and ignored Phil's triumphant sneer. She accepted Frank's business card and promised to give him a call if the PR department of the bank was interested in participating in the Christmas fund-raiser.

Lauren escorted her down the hall to the elevators. She pressed the button for Jac and scuffed the carpet with her foot as they waited for the car. "I'm sorry. I didn't mean to subject you to that."

"Shhh, it's not your fault. Sometimes I just rub people wrong."

Tears filled Lauren's eyes.

Jac impulsively pulled her into a hug. She held her for a moment as Lauren's arms tightened. "Hey, can you imagine how they'd have been if I'd brought a date?"

Lauren gave a short laugh and pulled away. Jac brushed a hand over her wet cheeks, pleased when the gesture elicited a wan smile. "No big deal, my friend. Now, you have a good night, and I'll give you a call later in the week, okay? We've been working hard. Maybe we can plan something fun soon."

The elevator arrived, and Jac entered. Turning, her gaze locked with Lauren's until the doors closed.

Poor kid. I feel like I'm leaving her alone in the snake pit. Jac fought an impulse to hit the stop button and return to Lauren's floor. *Yeah, right. Ride to the rescue. I'm sure that's exactly what she wants.*

Despondent, Jac left the building and walked to the cab stand, grateful to be out of the oppressive environment.

The senior Emersons left, and Lauren was still cleaning up in the kitchen when Phil came up from behind and wrapped his arms around her. She pushed him off and continued to load the dishwasher.

"C'mon, babe, that can wait for the morning. I'm sure we can find something more fun to do." He tried again to embrace her.

She pulled away and spun angrily. "You think after the way you behaved tonight that I have the least bit of interest in having sex with you?"

"What? What did I do?"

She stared at him incredulously. "You were a total jerk to my friend. I invited Jac tonight because I wanted you two to get to know each other. Now I wouldn't blame her if she never sets foot in this apartment again."

"Good. I don't want her here."

"What the hell is your problem? You've never even met her before tonight, and you act like she's your worst enemy."

"Look, you don't know everything about her."

"I know that she's a wonderful friend, that she's considerate and sweet and funny."

"She's a dyke."

Lauren shrugged. "I know she's gay. So what?"

Phil's jaw dropped and his eyes widened, but she was too livid to find anything comical in his reaction.

"You know?"

"I do. She told me the first night we went to the concert. She didn't want me to be uncomfortable. So, how did you know?"

Phil's gaze darted around the kitchen. "Uh, it's obvious just looking at her."

"No, it's not. Now, how did you know Jac is gay?"

Phil thrust his hands in his pockets and fidgeted. "I looked her up on Facebook, and Mom confirmed my suspicions."

"What? How the hell did your mother do that?"

Phil stared at the fridge and refused to meet Lauren's glare. "I dunno. Mom's got a lot of contacts around the city so she probably asked around." He held out a conciliatory hand. "She was just worried about you, and so am I. I'm afraid your...friend is brainwashing you. You haven't been yourself since you met her."

Lauren's nostrils flared. "I'm never more myself than when I'm with her. She doesn't try and put me in a pigeonhole like some people. And where the hell do you get off checking out my friends?"

"God, see what I mean? She's got you all messed up. I'm serious, Lauren. I do not want you to see her ever again."

"Did I just hear you forbid me to see my friend?"

Phil jutted out his chin. "Yes, I did. You're going to be my wife, Lauren."

She regarded him coldly. "Your wife, not your property. And frankly, I'm not even sure I want to be your wife anymore."

He gaped at her.

"Oh, and another thing. If you think I'm going to live in a house across the street from your mother, you and she are sadly mistaken. I would live on the street before I'd live in the old Carlton place."

He slammed his fist down on the counter. "Well, if you think we're going to the farm instead of the Marquettes' next Saturday, you're goddamned crazy."

She abandoned the cleanup. "I'm going to bed. Don't bother joining me."

"It's my home, and I'll sleep where I fucking well want!"

Ignoring his bellow, she stalked away, but she hadn't missed his turn of phrase. At that moment, though, she didn't care if it was ever *their* home again.

An hour later, Lauren stared at the ceiling above their bed. The dull roar of the TV echoed from the living room. *Wonder how long it'll take before the neighbours call the superintendent.*

She rubbed a hand over her eyes, wondering if she'd made a mistake accepting his proposal. He'd been sweet and persistent, but even at the time she'd been haunted by a sense that it was far too soon; they barely knew each other. It wasn't the first time she'd had her doubts, but now she allowed herself to pursue that train of thought. Phil had been jubilant when she finally said yes. His words echoed in her mind. "I'm so happy, Lauren. Dad said you'd be the making of me. He's right."

The memory of those words sent a shudder through her. Had he proposed because Frank and Phyllis disapproved of him drinking like a college kid and tearing around with his buddies? Her chest tightened. Frank hadn't promoted Phil to management until after they'd announced their engagement. Had her fiancé pushed so hard for their engagement because he desperately wanted off the sales floor?

Rolling onto her side, Lauren pulled a pillow over her ears and focused on quieting her mind, but sleep remained elusive.

The anger that had been lurking just below the surface flared. *So you won't go to see my family this weekend. Screw you. I'm going anyway.* She punched her pillow and glared at the door. *Jac would go see the family with me.*

She froze. *Would she?* She pictured Jac sitting at the crowded dinner table. *I'll bet Jason would challenge her to an arm wrestling match.* She chuckled at the thought. *She could hold her own.*

Her family wouldn't give a fig about Jac's orientation. They were already such a diverse group that one more oddity wouldn't faze them.

She imagined showing Jac around the farm, introducing her to Topsy, the ancient white mare that her father couldn't bear to put down, and pointing out where the hens hid their eggs in the hay.

She grabbed her phone off the nightstand and texted, *want 2 join my fam for an early thanksgiving on Saturday?*

The response came back within seconds. *Love to.*

Lauren smiled and tapped out her reply. *Gr8. will figure out details l8r. cya.*

Looking forward to it. Good night.

Lauren set the phone aside and breathed deeply to release some of the evening's tension. She had serious decisions to make, but not tonight. She'd wait until she was thinking more clearly.

Unable to sleep because of the cacophony coming from the other room, she picked up her phone again and cast a glance at the closed door. Phil was no doubt consoling himself with a six pack and would probably pass out in the recliner.

With a sigh, she went online and resumed a familiar search. Ever since Lauren had learned that Jac was a member at Sous-terre, she'd been doing cyber research. After sorting through the innumerable links to pornography that sprang up when she entered her search parameters, she'd found a number of fascinating sites that discussed everything from the history to the psychology to the practice of BDSM.

She'd had many questions answered in the last week, but now as she brought up one of the more scientific sites, she continued to ignore the one question she refused to ask herself or Google: Why did she find Jac's sexual proclivities so fascinating?

Chapter 10

BECCA TAPPED ON JAC'S OPEN office door. "There's someone here to see you. She didn't give her name and doesn't have an appointment, but she said to tell you that the boss wants to take you for dinner. Did you want me to show her in, or should I—"

Jac grinned. "Absolutely, show her in. She's a friend." It was an excellent ending to a bad day. She rose and moved from behind her desk as Lauren poked her head around the doorjamb. "Aren't you a sight for sore eyes? What brings you to my lair?"

"I decided this was the perfect day to pay you back for all the times you've fed me." Lauren looked around the well-appointed office. "Nice place you have here, underling."

Jac pulled up a chair for her guest. "Thanks, boss. I'm not complaining, but you did just feed me a superb dinner last night."

Lauren sighed. "The food might've been decent, but I don't think the company was up to par. I'd really like to take you out."

Jac took a seat next to Lauren and patted her hand. "You were there, so in my opinion, the company was as wonderful as the roast beef."

"Charmer."

"Just calling them like I see them. So how did you find my home-away-from-home? Did you have me followed?"

Lauren shook her head. "Nothing so cloak and dagger. Victoria told me how to get here. Hey, do you know if she's feeling all right? She looked all queasy and pale this afternoon again. It's not the first time, either. She looked ill a couple of times last week, too. She's not sick, is she?"

"Not that I know of. I haven't seen her for a while, but we've talked and texted, and she didn't mention any illness." Sadness settled into Jac's heart. *This isn't right...for any of us. But how the hell do I get out of it? I really don't want to have to make good on Vic's wager. I need to figure out how to approach her, how to convince her to just call this off.*

"Are *you* okay? You don't look so hot either."

Jac forced a smile. "I'm fine. It's just been one of those Mondays, you know?"

"God, yes. That's why I'm here to kidnap you away."

"Give me five minutes to wrap things up, and then I'm all yours." Jac returned to her desk, shut down several open files, and checked her calendar for the next day's appointments. "Okay, we can go."

They left the office, and Jac waved to Becca. "See you tomorrow."

Becca nodded. "Have a good evening."

When they got in the elevator, Lauren said, "Your assistant is very protective of you, isn't she? I wasn't sure she'd take my message in without me undergoing a DNA scan first."

"Becca's a great assistant, actually. And now that she knows you're a friend, you'll have free access—no ID required."

"Good. Because I think I'll make a habit of this."

Jac smiled. "All right, but you're only allowed to buy dinner this one time."

Lauren leaned into Jac. "We'll talk."

The elevator opened and they exited, laughing.

"So did you have a place in mind?" Jac asked.

"I do. I found this little hole-in-the-wall diner about a week after I moved here—"

"Dingle's Diner?"

Lauren glanced at Jac. "You know it?"

"Know it? I practically lived there my first year of gainful employment." Jac wrapped an arm around Lauren's shoulders and gave her a quick hug. "Perfect choice. I haven't been there in ages."

"Excellent."

A short walk brought them to the diner, and they lucked into the last available table. Jac was delighted to see that the menu hadn't changed, and she ordered an old favourite.

"I'm going to have to run an extra couple of miles tomorrow morning to work this off, but it'll be worth it."

Lauren ordered the same. "I know. Nothing beats an old-fashioned, homemade burger, fries, and shake, does it? And speaking of old-fashioned, I hope you've got your taste buds ready for this weekend. Mom's going all out for our pre-Thanksgiving dinner."

"I'm really looking forward to it, but why is she having it this weekend instead of actually on Thanksgiving?"

"Because with eight of us, it's too hard to get everyone home on Thanksgiving. After Brian got married and Anjali, Courtney, and Adam moved to Edmonton, Mom instituted pre-Thanksgiving. That way everyone gets to share our family celebration and still uphold other commitments on the actual holiday. Brian goes to his in-laws, and my sisters in Edmonton get to spend it with their significant others. It works really well for us."

"Are you sure there'll be room for me?"

"Absolutely. There was a place for Phil, and since he's not going—"

"I'm sorry."

Lauren shook her head. "No, please don't worry about it. We're having an issue at the moment, but this is just one of those couple things. We'll work it out."

"Are you sure? I don't want to cause—"

Lauren sat up straight and levelled a stern look at Jac. "You're not. As I said, we have some things to work out, but they're about us, not anything else."

Jac toyed with her spoon and stared at the table, feeling like the biggest hypocrite in the world.

Lauren's hand settled over Jac's, stilling its movement. "Hey. It's okay."

Jac met Lauren's gaze. "Is it? Are you okay?"

She hesitated. "Yes and no. We had a big fight last night, and this morning we picked right up where we left off."

"Is that why you wanted to go for dinner with me?"

"That's part of it. I really like hanging out with you, but yes, I'm avoiding going home until I have to." Lauren snorted. "I don't know why I bother, though. He texted that he was going with his friends tonight to some sports bar, so it's not like he'll be home before midnight. But I decided I'd rather enjoy some good company than mope around the apartment all evening."

"I'm glad. And if you want to come over and hang out at the loft after dinner, you're more than welcome."

"Thanks. I might take you up on that."

It occurred to Jac that with a little effort this could be the night for her to win the bet, but she pushed the thought aside. *No, not like this.* "So, tell me about your family. If I'm going to meet everyone this weekend, I'd like to have an in-depth briefing first."

Lauren smiled. "All right, but you may want to take notes. There's a lot to tell. So, my parents are Cynthia and Steven. I told you about Mom being a handywoman extraordinaire, but I didn't tell you about my dad. He works every bit as hard as Mom, but he's the softest touch you'll ever meet…"

Jac gazed out the window as they drove down the back road. "This is beautiful countryside. Especially at this time of year."

Lauren grinned. "Isn't it? I loved growing up as a farm kid."

"Did all your siblings feel like that?"

"Jason did. He still lives here. He and Dad work together, and I expect some day he'll inherit the place."

"And the others?"

"Well, it's the only home Zac and Sara have ever known, since they came to us as babies." Lauren slowed as they passed the Andersons' mailbox. She was eager to see everyone, but she'd been enjoying their conversation on the drive up from the city and wasn't in a hurry to end it. "I know Mom and Dad worry about what will happen to them once they go, but the rest of us, we'll look after them." *Even if I have to work around Phil to do my part.*

"And the ones in Edmonton?"

"I don't think they'd ever come back to live in the country. They're like me—they love to come home for visits, but they're citified now."

"So you'd never live outside the city again?"

Lauren shot Jac a wry glance. "Do you have any idea how long I worked on Phil just to get him to visit the farm? He'd have a heart attack if I suggested we move outside city limits."

"Are things…okay, now? You were pretty upset Monday night."

Warmth surged up Lauren's neck. "I'm really sorry. I didn't mean to literally cry on your shoulder like that.

You probably had to wring your shirt out and swab the floors by the time I went home."

Jac touched Lauren's arm. "Please, don't apologize. That's not what I meant at all. I just...well, I half-expected you to text me by this morning that Phil had changed his mind, and he was going with you instead. Not that I'm not delighted to be with you, but...I just wondered if things got any better later in the week."

Lauren sighed and shook her head. "Not really, no. He wouldn't budge, and for once I refused to cave in. It's sort of been like living in Siberia this week, though there's been a few times I thought for sure the neighbours would call the police on us."

"Are you safe?" Jac studied her. "I'm serious."

"Oh, it's not as bad as all that. Just a little screaming." *At the top of our lungs.* "Phil would never hit me." Lauren glanced at Jac, whose brow was creased. "Really. I'm fine. My relationship might be a bit ragged at the moment, and Wednesday wasn't exactly fun. I refused to go look at the Carlton house with him and his mother. He lost it and stormed out of the apartment. I didn't see him again until Friday morning. Anyway, I'm not going to think about that today, all right? I'm going to enjoy seeing my whole family, and showing you around the farm, and having one of Mom's fabulous dinners. Tomorrow is another day."

Jac smiled. "That's very Scarlett O'Hara of you."

"Just don't expect me to wear curtains." Lauren turned into her parents' driveway. "Oh, it looks like everyone else is already here."

"Good, I'm so looking forward to meeting them. I brought something for your nephews—is that okay? I know you have a Tootsie Pop thing going with them, and I don't want to interfere."

The misery of the last week with Phil vanished in the warmth engendered by Jac's thoughtfulness. "Absolutely. If it's something sweet, they'll be your friends forever."

As Lauren parked the car, most of her family spilled out of the front door. Jacob and Nick led the way, hurtling toward Lauren as she stepped out of the car. Laughing, she knelt and wrapped her arms around them.

"Bring us, bring us?" Nick said.

"Did you, Auntie? Did you bring us something?" Jacob asked.

"Well, actually, my friend Jac brought you something." Lauren looked up at Jac with a smile. The boys clung to Lauren as Jac knelt and pulled two huge all-day suckers out of her pocket. Their eyes widened, and Nick grabbed for one.

"Wow!" Jacob accepted his candy. "That's the biggest one I've ever seen."

They scampered back to show their parents as Lauren was swarmed by the others. Amidst gales of laughter, hugs, and kisses, she managed to greet each of them.

Then she turned to Jac and pulled her forward. "Everyone, I want you to meet my friend, Jac Lanier." She rattled off everyone's names, and Jac returned Sara's hug and shook hands with the others.

Sara tugged on Jac's arm. "Tippy had puppies. Want to see them?"

Bitter Fruit

"I'd love to see them." Jac followed Sara as she led the way around the house toward the barn. Jacob and Nick ran after them.

"Will your friend be all right?" Cynthia asked as she linked arms with her daughter for the walk up the pathway. "Did you want to go after them?"

"I will once I say hi to Zac, but she'll be okay. She's good with people."

"I was a little surprised when you told me you'd be bringing a friend instead of Phillip—not that she's not welcome, of course."

"Trust me, right now she's a lot better company than Phil." Lauren sighed and leaned into her mother.

"Troubles?"

"You could say that. We'll talk about it later, okay?"

"Of course. Ah, there are your brothers now."

Jason wheeled Zac out the door and down the ramp. Lauren jogged over to hug both of them.

Twenty minutes later, after preliminary catch-ups and fending off inquiries from Anjali, Courtney, and Adam about Phil, Lauren excused herself and walked back to the barn. The soft sound of voices came from inside, and after a quick peek, Lauren pulled out her phone to capture the moment.

Nick sat on Jac's lap, sucker in one hand, petting a puppy with the other. Sara and Jacob each held one of Tippy's brood, and all four seemed completely absorbed in the moment as Tippy kept her eye on them. Lauren's heart melted as she snapped the photo. *Yeah, you rub people wrong—sure you do. Busted, you big old softie. You're as bad as Dad.*

Jacob glanced up. "Auntie, look! Their eyes are open now."

Lauren joined them and sat next to Jac, accepting the puppy Sara handed to her.

Jac shot her an abashed grin. "Sorry, I didn't mean to abandon you."

"Not at all. I'm glad you got to see the puppies."

"Tippy's a good mommy," Sara said.

"I'll bet she is, sweetie. Her puppies are certainly adorable." Lauren held the border collie pup up to eye level. "You got lucky, didn't you?" She turned to Jac. "Tippy was abandoned on our road and Dad took her in, pregnant and all."

"Grandpa does that all the time," Jacob said. "Do you think he'll let us keep the puppies, Auntie?"

Lauren shook her head. "I don't think we have room for any more dogs, but maybe if you ask your mom and dad, they'll let you have a puppy once they're old enough to leave Tippy."

Jacob set the puppy down and scrambled to his feet. Nick followed, and they ran out of the barn as fast as little legs could carry them.

Jac laughed. "Why do I get the feeling that Brian and Andrea are not going to be thrilled with you?"

Lauren winked at her. "Jakie will bat his big blue eyes at them and Nicky will do his happy dance all around them, and they'll cave in a heartbeat. And if not, Dad will find good homes for the pups. He always finds homes for the dogs abandoned out here, or we end up keeping them." She rose to her feet. "Come meet the oldest animal resident of Blaine farm."

"Okay." Jac brushed off the hay as she got to her feet. "Sara, do you want to come with us?"

Sara shook her head and gathered another puppy into her lap. "I want to play with Tippy's babies."

"All right, sweetie. We'll see you back at the house, okay?" Lauren asked.

"Uh-huh."

They'd reached the barn door when Sara said, "I like you, Jac."

"I like you, too, Sara."

My sister is a very good judge of character. Lauren elbowed Jac with a grin. "Looks like you made a great first impression."

"Suckers and puppies—how could I go wrong?"

"True. Speaking of which, where did you find those all-days? I haven't seen them around since I was little."

"I got restless Thursday after work, so I went for a drive and ended up in Nanton. I couldn't resist going to The Candy Store. I'm addicted to their coffee crunch candies, and when I saw those, I thought of your nephews."

"The Candy Store?"

"Yeah. Have you never been there?"

Lauren shook her head.

"I'll have to take you sometime. It's only about an hour south of the city, and it's this wonderful old-fashioned candy store. They're colocated with an antique store and an ice cream parlour. I could spend hours there, just browsing and eating."

"It sounds fabulous. You should've called me."

Jac stopped and faced Lauren. "I thought of it. I'd have loved to have you along, but I didn't want to cause any more trouble between you and Phil."

Lauren grimaced. "Phil and I aren't joined at the hip, you know. He has his friends, and I have—" *You.* "And I have the right to see other people, too. Next time, at least text me, okay? If we've got plans, I'll let you know, but it never hurts to ask."

"Okay, boss. Next time my sweet tooth or wanderlust acts up, I'll let you know."

"Good. I'm glad that's settled." Lauren stopped in front of a corral where an elderly white mare was grazing. "I want you to meet Topsy. I've known her all my life, and all of us kids learned to ride on her. Even Zac's ridden with Dad behind him."

"How old is she?"

"She'll be thirty next spring."

Lauren leaned on the railing and whistled. Topsy's head came up, and she ambled across the corral to have her nose petted. "Hey, old girl. I want you to meet a friend of mine. Sorry I didn't bring you anything this time."

Jac reached in her jacket pocket and came out with an apple. "Would it be okay to give her this?"

Lauren's eyebrows rose. "Good heavens, is your coat like Mary Poppins' satchel? What else would I find in there?"

Jac laughed and shook her head. "I just figured we'd be visiting Topsy at some point, so when I left with Sara, I swiped it off the ground in the backyard."

"Damn, is there anything you don't think of?" Lauren was charmed by Jac's blush. "Go ahead. She'll love it. You're going to have everyone eating out of your hand by the end of this visit. Literally."

Jac held the apple out on the palm of her hand.

Topsy took it and finished it in several bites. She turned sideways to them, and they reached through the railing to pat her flanks. When she wandered away, they swung up to the top rail and sat watching her.

"She's quite portly, isn't she? Or is that normal? I really know nothing about horses. The closest I ever came to them is when I took a date for a carriage ride in Montreal once."

Lauren shifted uncomfortably. *Oh, for heaven's sake. So she took a date on a romantic carriage ride. It's no business of yours.*

"Topsy's actually been as broad as a barn door for as long as I can remember. When I rode her as a kid, my legs would stick straight out from the saddle because they weren't long enough to go around her belly."

Jac grinned. "As a kid, eh? When was that—two years ago?"

Lauren elbowed Jac. "Funny, funny lady...not."

The sun warmed their backs as they sat quietly, arms touching as their hands rested on the rail. Lauren closed her eyes and allowed the last of the stressful week to fade away. *Right here, right now, everything's okay. Tippy and her pups, Topsy, Jakie, Nick... They all worked their magic like I knew they would. And you, my friend... you've got magic in your pockets, too.*

Chapter 11

Lauren rose to help her mother and sisters clear the table. Jac started to stand too, but Lauren put a hand on her shoulder. "No, that's okay. First time here, you have guest privileges. You stay and defend Calgary's honour."

Jason snorted. "What honour? Calgary's the city of losers. Edmonton is the city of champions."

Jac leaned forward with a grin. "Champions? When was the last time the Eskimos even got to the Grey Cup?"

Cries of outrage went up from Jason, Brian, and Adam.

"We pretty much owned it in the eighties and nineties," Jason said. "It's only been nine years since we last won."

"Well, we took it six years ago, so it's clear who has the better team."

Adam pointed at Jac. "Hah! You lost the big game in 2012 and choked so bad last year you never even made it past the semifinals."

"At least we got into the semifinals," Jac shot back.

Lauren entered the kitchen with an armload of dishes. In the eternal battle of Calgary versus Edmonton, Jac was in enemy territory, but she'd held her own all through dinner. This despite the concerted efforts of Lauren's brothers to get her to admit Edmonton's superiority in everything from culture to universities, business to politics, and their favourite arena, sports.

"Your friend isn't easily intimidated, is she?" Anjali asked.

"Not so you'd notice." Lauren set her stack of dishes on the counter.

"I think Adam's got a bit of a crush on her," Courtney said. "Have you noticed the way he can't keep his eyes off her?"

What? Lauren's brow furrowed. "She's out of his league. Besides, she's gay. She's not going to give old Don Juan there a second look."

"She is?" Courtney chortled. "Excellent. I'm so going to torture Adam all the way back to Edmonton."

Good. He deserves it, though I can't really blame him for looking. "Are you guys heading back tonight or staying over?"

Courtney elbowed Anjali. "Are you kidding? Do you think this one could be away from *Jeffy* for more than a few hours?"

"It's Jeffrey, as he's told you a thousand times." Anjali beamed as she glanced at her engagement ring. "But I have to plead guilty. I miss him so much when he's not around. I wish he hadn't had to work today, but interns are slaves to the hospital. At least he gets Thanksgiving off, so we'll see his family then."

Lauren's smile faded, and she busied herself loading dishes in the washer.

"Will you girls finish up here?" Cynthia asked. "I want to have a word with your sister."

Lauren looked up and intercepted an unspoken communication between her mom, Courtney, and Anjali. "Mom?"

"Come sit on the back porch with me for a bit, hon."

Lauren glanced toward the dining room.

"Don't worry about Jac. She's fine."

They sat on the back step and fended off the dogs as they ran up in anticipation of treats. "Get down, Maxie. Good girl." Cynthia pushed the chocolate lab's nose aside as a three-legged springer spaniel tried to shove his way past and a Chihuahua squirmed under the taller dogs. "Off you go, Farley. Bilbo, you know better than that." She pointed toward the barn. "You know where your supper dishes are, and I happen to know Sara filled them before we sat down."

The dogs ran off, Maxie well in the lead, and Cynthia patted Lauren's hand.

"Okay, you. What's going on?"

Lauren didn't meet her mother's gaze. "What do you mean?"

"Your face fell like a lead balloon when Anjali talked about Jeffrey. Not to mention that Phil's not here, when I very specifically remember you telling me weeks ago that he'd be coming up with you."

Lauren hung her head. "Things are kind of rough between us right now, Mom. And I don't know what to do about it."

"What do you mean 'rough'? Has he harmed you in any way?"

"That's what Jac asked, too. No, Mom, Phil raises his voice, not his fists."

"I don't particularly care for the sound of that either."

"Mom, you know you and Dad argue too."

"Of course. We've been together for almost forty years. We'd have to be saints never to be upset with each other, and neither of us are saints. But, honey, I get a feeling this isn't just about routine arguments. Something feels really off to me. You don't feel…happy to me. You haven't for a long time."

"I'm not happy." *Except when I'm hanging out with Jac.* Lauren's eyes filled, and she brushed at the tears. "I think I screwed up, Mom. I think it might've been a mistake accepting Phil's proposal."

Her mother was quiet.

"Please, tell me what you're thinking. Do you think I made a mistake?"

Cynthia sighed. "You know I try not to interfere in you kids' lives. You have the right to make choices, and if sometimes those choices are mistakes—"

"So you do think I made a mistake."

"I didn't say that."

Lauren fought the urge to shake her mother. "Yes, you did. You said I had the right to make a mistake, so you must think Phil was a mistake. Do the others think so, too?"

"I don't want to speak for your siblings, hon, but your sisters have been worried. They said when they call or Skype lately, you seem…stressed."

"So they think I screwed up, too."

"I didn't say that either. But maybe you did rush into the engagement a little bit. You'd only known Phil a few months when he proposed."

"You always say you knew Dad was the one the first time he took you to a school dance."

"True, but he didn't propose until four years later, so I had time to learn who he really was and fall so deeply in love that even all these years later, through good times and bad, I can't imagine my life without him. Can you imagine your life without Phil?"

Lauren toyed with her engagement ring. "I don't know. When Anjali talks about Jeffrey, her whole face lights up. It's clear she's crazy about him. I just don't know, Mom. I don't know if I feel that for Phil."

Cynthia put her arm around Lauren. "Then I think that's what you have to figure out. Just remember that you haven't done anything irrevocable. If this engagement is a mistake, it's not the end of the world. Your family will always love you, and your friends will understand."

"Aside from Victoria, my only other friend is sitting in there, arguing sports with my brothers."

Cynthia canted her head. "What do you mean? I thought you had lots of friends in the city. Heaven knows you always did when you worked in town here."

"I hang out with a bunch of people, but the women are mostly girlfriends of Phil's buddies. I don't really consider them my friends. To me, a friend is someone whose ear you can talk off and you never run out of conversation. They're there for you through thick and thin. They've always got your back, no matter what."

"Is Jac that kind of friend?"

God knows I can cry on her shoulder. She proved that last week. "She really is. You know, she's only been in my life for a few weeks, but I feel like I've known her forever."

Cynthia laughed. "You do seem to be on the same wavelength. I think Adam was jealous of the way you kept finishing each other's sentences."

Lauren rolled her eyes. "I'd love to see his face when Courtney clues him in on the ride home."

"Your sister does take inordinate delight in teasing the poor boy."

"Poor boy? Are we talking about the same guy who put frogs in my and Anjali's bed when we were ten? Who glued Brian's hockey sticks together? Who substituted baking soda for baking powder when you were making cakes for the Fall Fair? That Adam?"

"He does hold his own pretty well, doesn't he?"

"No kidding." *I don't want to go home tonight.* "Mom…"

"Yes, dear?"

"Would it be okay if we stayed the night? I haven't asked Jac, and we didn't bring so much as a toothbrush, but if she's good with it, is it okay with you?"

"Of course, anytime. It's still your home, too. You can take your old room. I'm sure I can round up a couple of toothbrushes for you, and you know I've never broken the habit of buying groceries by the bushel."

Lauren rose to her feet. "You're the best. I'm going to ask Jac. And, Mom, thanks. I'm not making any decisions tonight, but I have a lot of things to think about."

"I'm glad. Just remember we love you, okay?"

"Always."

Lauren returned to the kitchen where Anjali, Courtney, and Sara were finishing up the cleaning. Anjali shot her a sympathetic glance.

"Everything okay?" Courtney asked.

Lauren nodded. "It will be. Maybe not today, but... Thanks."

Hoots of laughter resounded from the dining room. Male voices chanted, "Jac, Jac, Jac..."

The sisters scrambled to the doorway to see what was going on.

Jac and Adam each had a bottle tipped to their mouth, guzzling beer. Jac slammed hers down first and wiped her mouth.

Steven clicked a stopwatch and held it up for all to see.

Jason grabbed Jac's arm and raised it. "We have a winner! Three in twenty-eight seconds flat. Adam, you wuss, you've met your match."

Brian elbowed Adam. "Nicky could chug faster than you."

Anjali rolled her eyes. "Time to tear Adam away and hit the road, or we'll be pouring him into the car by the time we leave."

Cries of protest went up when Anjali and Courtney seized Adam and pulled him from Jac's side.

Lauren approached Jac, put her hands on her shoulders, and leaned down to whisper. "Got a minute?"

Jac burped and covered her mouth. "Oops, sorry. It's all Adam's fault. He challenged me, and I couldn't say no."

Lauren smiled. "Of course not."

Jac shot her a sheepish look. Lauren beckoned Jac to follow her down the hall. The bedroom hadn't changed much since she and Anjali had shared it. Their twin beds were still on opposite sides of the room, and the dresser still stood near the window—but it was much neater than they'd always left it.

"So I was wondering... I know this is short notice, and I completely understand if you want to say no..."

Jac gave her a lopsided grin. "To you, never. What's up, short stuff?"

Lauren raised an eyebrow. "Exactly how many beers did you two have?"

"Three. And I kicked Adam's ass. But I did have an unfair advantage." Jac chuckled.

"What? Did you puncture the can first or something?"

"Nuh-uh. Anyway, what were you saying?"

"Oh, right. Would you mind if we stayed here tonight rather than going back to the city?"

Jac rubbed her belly. "Sure, as long as no one challenges me to another chugging contest. Three's my limit at the best of times, and I'm so full right now I couldn't fit a glass of water down there."

"Well, the Edmonton trio are leaving in a few minutes, so you should be safe. Mom said she has spare toiletries. I keep some things here, and maybe I can borrow one of Dad's T-shirts for you to sleep in."

"Don't worry about it. I never wear anything to bed." Jac glanced at her. "Um, unless that would bother you."

Lauren bit her lip. "Of course not."

Jac followed her back into the hall. "Your mom is so nice. Your whole family is great. I've had a wonderful time."

"I'm glad. I thought tomorrow we could take a walk around the farm, maybe burn off Mom's dinner before we head home."

"Sounds good. There's nothing pressing I have to get back for. No one's waiting for me."

Me either. Lauren shook her head. *Now, stop that right there. Of course Phil will be waiting for you. Which reminds me, I'd better let him know I won't be home until tomorrow.*

"Lauren? Is everything all right?"

"Of course. Why do you ask?"

"Because you're making a pretty fierce face. You look like you're about to go into battle."

Only metaphorically. "No, everything's fine. I just have to give Phil a quick call. I'll catch up with you, okay?"

"Sure." Jac ambled down the hall.

Lauren returned to the bedroom and took out her phone. She'd turned it off when she left their apartment and half-expected it to buzz with multiple messages when it came on, but there weren't any. She chewed her lip for a moment, then sent a quick text to Phil. *Staying w/folks 2nite. CU tomorrow.*

She shut off the phone and rejoined her family.

While Jac used the washroom, Lauren sat on her childhood bed and checked her phone. There were still no messages from Phil, though Anjali had sent one.

Tell Mom home safe. Adam swallowed tongue. Can't believe Jac is gay. LOL

Lauren grinned and her fingers flew. *Tell Adam will mail eyeballs back l8r.*

Anjali's answer came moments later. *2 late. No need for i's. His heart is crushed.*

Jac came back into the room. "What's so funny?"

"My siblings. Anjali was just letting me know they're home safely." Lauren shut the phone back off. *No midnight calls tonight, thank you very much.* "Back in a moment."

When Lauren returned from the bathroom, Jac's clothes were on a chair, and she was in Anjali's old bed with the covers drawn up, arms folded under her head as she looked out the window.

Lauren shut off the ceiling light, but left her bedside lamp on until she'd slid between the covers.

"I really want to thank you again for today. I don't remember the last time I had so much fun. Your family is a hoot."

"They think you're pretty great, too. You know Adam has a little crush on you, right?"

"I recognized the signs. Should I be concerned?"

"Not at all. Courtney and Anjali enlightened him on the drive home, and took devilish delight in doing so."

Jac laughed.

"So what did you mean earlier when you said you had an advantage over him in the chugging contest?"

Jac's laughter trailed off. "One more tale from my sordid past, I'm afraid."

Lauren rolled to face her. "How sordid?"

"Not too, but I did drink pretty heavily in my university days, at least for the first couple of years until I smartened up. I used to take great delight in beating the frat boys at their own game, and I mastered shotgunning a glass without actually swallowing, just pouring it down my throat. I haven't done it for a lot of years, but it came back to me fast tonight."

"Still, it was pretty impressive. Adam's not exactly a teetotaller."

"It was kind of juvenile, but they made me feel like one of the—"

"Family."

"I was going to say 'the guys,' but yes, they all made me feel right at home." Jac yawned loudly. "All this wonderful country air. I'm going to sleep like a log tonight."

"Really? You're used to a king. I would think sleeping in a twin would be a trial."

"Nothing can ruin this day, not even sleeping in a midget's bed."

"Hey!"

Jac chuckled. "I'm sorry. Is that not the *au courant* term for you little people?"

Lauren hurled a pillow across the room.

Jac turned to the wall to avoid it, her back a pale flash in the moonlight.

Lauren's breath caught, and she rolled away. When the pillow sailed back in her direction, she barely noticed. They settled down, and Jac's breathing began to deepen.

After some long moments, Lauren whispered, "Jac? Are you awake?"

"Mmm-hmm."

Lauren hesitated.

Jac faced her. "What's up?"

"Have you...no, never mind. Sorry I bothered you. G'night."

"Didn't I tell you that you could ask me anything? What's going on in your head?" Amusement shimmered in Jac's voice.

Lauren's heart pounded. "It really is no business of mine."

"S'okay. Ask anyway."

"I was just wondering...have you been to Sous-terre lately?"

Jac didn't hesitate. "I dropped by last night for an hour or so."

"Oh."

"Does that bother you?"

"No, of course not." *Hot and bothered, maybe.* "I was just curious about how often you go."

"There's no set schedule. Members drop by when they feel like it. I usually go several times a month."

"So...you don't know who might be there to, um, play with?"

"Not unless I've made plans with someone beforehand."

Lauren closed her eyes. "Do you usually do that? I mean, is there someone in particular you like to be with there?"

"I have my favourites—women who I'm always glad to see, but if you mean any sort of committed relationships, then no. The whole idea of the club is to experience nonexclusive sex."

"Hmmm."

Jac yawned again. "Why do you ask?"

"No reason, just curious."

"Okay. Have a good sleep. I'll see you in the morning."

"Goodnight, Jac."

Jac shuffled around until she faced the wall. Almost immediately her breathing deepened again. Sleep was much slower to come for Lauren as her imagination worked overtime. She longed to touch herself, but didn't dare for fear of waking Jac. *God, that would be so embarrassing.*

By the time her mind quieted enough to permit slumber, Lauren was exhausted.

Chapter 12

When Lauren awoke, sunlight filled the bedroom. She yawned, stretched, and opened her eyes.

Jac gazed at her from the other bed. "Good morning, sunshine. Did you sleep well?"

"When I finally got to sleep, I did." Lauren twisted to see the bedside clock. "Nine thirty? Wow. I never sleep in past eight thirty."

"It must be the air around here, because I'm never still in bed this late either."

"Been awake long?"

Jac sniffed the air. "Long enough to smell coffee brewing. I think at least your parents are up."

Lauren sat up and swung her feet out of bed. "It's Sunday. They'll be off to church with Sara and Zac in an hour. They usually go out for lunch after services, so I'll go say bye in case we leave before they get home."

"You did promise me a walk around the place."

"I did. How about a shower, breakfast, a walk, and then we'll head back to the city?"

Jac sat up and the covers fell away from her body. "Sounds good. Is it okay if I take the first shower? I'll be quick."

Lauren scrambled to her feet. "Sure. No hurry." She went out into the hall and turned to close the door. Jac was leaning over the bed to pull up and straighten the covers.

Lauren shut the door and exhaled deeply. *Okay, 'nuff of that, you peeping Tomasina.*

By the time she returned from the kitchen and a conversation with her family, Jac was getting dressed. Her damp hair still hung in loose waves.

"Did you find everything you need?" Lauren gathered her clothes.

"Do you know if there's a blow-dryer around? It's probably not a great idea to go for a hike with wet hair in this cold."

Lauren nodded. "There's one in the linen closet. I'll get it for you."

"That's okay. You go ahead and jump in the shower."

"Bottom shelf on the right. See you in a few." Lauren went into the bathroom, stripped down, and entered the glassed-in shower stall.

A moment later, there was a tap at the door, and then it opened a crack. "Do you mind if I dry my hair while you shower? There's no outlet by the bedroom mirror."

"Sure, go ahead." Lauren washed her hair while she watched Jac tame her locks. *This feels so...domestic.* She finished showering just as Jac unplugged the dryer's cord. When she slid the shower door open partway, Jac hastened to hold out a towel. "Wow, I have to come back to this hotel more often. The service here is great."

Jac winked. "Just don't forget to tip the maid, or there'll be no chocolate on your pillow tonight. Do you want the dryer, or should I put it away?"

Lauren stepped out of the stall with the towel wrapped around her. "Leave it, thanks. There's fresh coffee in the kitchen and a stack of French toast keeping warm in the oven. Help yourself."

"Mmm, sounds great. I'm going to have to go for an extra-long run tonight to make up for how well your mom's fed me this weekend."

"Actually, Dad makes Sunday breakfasts. I'll ask him to make us Spanish omelets the next time you're here. They're fabulous."

"I'd like that. See you in the kitchen." Jac slipped out of the bathroom.

Lauren finished drying and dressing, then faced her image in the mirror with a serious expression. "What does it say when you're looking forward to bringing your best friend home again more than you are your fiancé?"

It says something is very, very wrong. This isn't fair to Phil. You've got to make a decision...and soon.

Rimed with frost, the grass crackled underfoot as Lauren and Jac crossed the fields. Lauren breathed deeply of the crisp air. Her earlier angst was vanquished by the sunshine. *This really is the best time of year.* She pointed off to their right. "You know the small creek we crossed when we left the house?"

"Yes?"

"It widens over there behind those trees. We swam there in the summer and skated in the winter. I couldn't begin to tell you how many pucks we lost along the snowbanks."

"But you found them in the spring, right?"

"Most of them, but every Christmas, Mom and Dad would put a bucket of pucks under the tree as a Santa gift to all of us. By spring, there would only be a handful left."

Jac's gaze rose to follow the path of a flock of geese flying in formation overhead. "Maybe a Canada goose built his bride a mansion made of rubber from all those lost pucks."

"It could be their summer home, where they raise their goslings before heading south again."

"And they'd have a picket fence around it, built from splintered hockey sticks." Jac grinned. "I'm guessing there were a few of those."

Lauren laughed. "No kidding. The boys saved their good ones for organized games, so our pickup games were usually played with sticks held together with tape and chewing gum. Adam was the worst. He was always showing off, blasting slap shots at whoever was unlucky enough to get stuck as goalie. His sticks would literally fall apart on the ice. One time, Sara broke her nose when her skates got tripped up by a wood shard he left behind."

"You really did have an idyllic childhood, didn't you?"

"We had our troubles, like any family." Lauren focused on the uneven ground. "Alex, one of the kids we fostered, died after a school dance when he and some friends were riding in the bed of a truck. They were drunk, and he fell out and smashed his head on a rock. Mom was devastated. It was a tough time."

Jac draped an arm around Lauren's shoulders and hugged her. "I'm sorry."

Lauren glanced at Jac, whose gaze was warm with compassion and sympathy. "He wasn't with us long, and to tell you the truth, me and Anjali were kind of scared of him. We started locking our door at night."

"Did your parents know that?"

Lauren shook her head. "No, but we sure felt guilty after he died, because we'd been wishing he would go away."

Jac's arm fell away. "You know your wishes had nothing to do with his death, right?"

Lauren rolled her shoulders. "I know that now, but when you're eight years old, logic can be elusive."

They hiked through several fields and soon crested a small rise. Ahead of them was an old two-story house, its boards grey and warped. There was no glass in the windows, and holes were visible in the ceiling. Tall grasses surrounded the place, and glimpses of the prairie beyond could be seen through gaps in the walls at one end.

"That was my great-grandparents' home. They homesteaded here at the turn of the last century. This land has been passed down through four generations."

Jac studied the building. "It's kind of sad, isn't it? Without people, it's of no use anymore. It speaks to broken dreams and scattered families."

"Really? I don't see it that way at all."

"How do you see it, Miss Incurable Optimist?" Jac's eyes sparkled with mirth.

"Ha ha. Very funny. Got your head stuck in storm clouds up there, do you? Can't see any rainbows? Well, I think the echoes of love and laughter still live inside those walls. Those times are over, sure, but that's okay. The house sheltered its family through many storms and did its job proudly. That doesn't die, even if the house is long past its better days."

"You know it's an inanimate object, right?"

"Of course, but I genuinely think houses retain the vibrations of the families that lived within. When Phil and I were looking at one house, I got a bad feeling as soon as I walked inside. I couldn't get out of there fast enough even though Phil liked it. I found out later that a murder had taken place there many years before."

"You don't really think the house, what…absorbed the violence?"

"I do." Lauren stopped and faced Jac. "What did you feel when you walked into my parents' house?"

Jac looked off in the direction of the farmhouse. "I guess…warmth. It's a really comfortable place to be, very inviting."

"And that's what I felt when I walked into your loft, tacky furniture, and all." *And it's what I don't feel at the apartment.*

Jac's shoulders slumped. "I don't know that there's been much of a positive nature that my walls could absorb."

"Don't say that."

"It's true. No family, not a lot of friends around. Lots of sex, very little love. God, what an indictment of my life."

Lauren reached for Jac's hand and squeezed it. "Stop that. There's the warmth of you in those walls...the real you."

Jac looked away. "I'm not sure that you know the real me."

"I think I do, but even if I don't, I will eventually, and I sure like what I know already." Lauren tugged Jac toward the house. "Come on. Let's go explore."

"Are you sure it's safe?"

"They built homes to last a century ago. We used to play in here all the time when we were kids."

They stopped at the front entrance, where a door hung off rusted hinges at a lopsided angle. Lauren let go of Jac's hand to push the door to one side. It creaked, but moved easily. Enough sunlight penetrated through windows and various holes in the walls to illuminate the interior.

Jac stepped past Lauren to where something jutted out from behind a broken board. She tugged gently and a yellowed newspaper emerged. "Wow, look at the date on this thing. May 1915." She took it over to an open window, squinted, and whistled softly. "*Steamer Lusitania torpedoed and sunk off Irish coast. 2000 on-*

board. Only 650 saved. Damn, I'm holding a real piece of history here."

She turned the paper over and laughed. "This ad is really cool. *Palmolive soap. Appeals to Dainty Women.*" She showed Lauren the picture of two women sitting together in night clothing on a bed. One held a book out to the other. "Who knew they had LGBT-friendly advertising back then? I just might have to switch soap brands."

She started to put the paper back where she'd found it, but Lauren stopped her. "You can take it with you if you want. It was probably just insulation to them."

"Are you sure? It could be valuable, and it belongs to your family."

Lauren shrugged. "You found it. I doubt anyone comes here anymore. I can't see Brian and Andrea permitting the boys to roam this far. Keep it."

Jac tucked the newspaper under her arm. "Thank you. So what's upstairs?"

"Four bedrooms. You wouldn't believe how small the closets are. I couldn't get a fraction of my wardrobe in them, and they probably had two or three people sharing a room."

"Is it safe to go up there?"

"It was. You should be fine if you watch your step. I'm going to check the kitchen. There used to be an antique kettle we played with long ago. If it's still there, I think I'll take it home with me."

The old iron kettle was still there, on its side in a corner. Delighted, she picked it up. "Hey, Jac, I found—"

There was a shriek from the second floor and the clatter of running footsteps on the stairs. Lauren bolted from the kitchen. Jac dashed out the front door with Lauren hard on her heels. They stopped twenty metres from the house, gasping for air.

"What the hell was that?" Lauren tried to catch her breath. "It sounded like the hounds of hell were after you?"

"Bats."

"Bats?"

Jac nodded, her chest heaving. "Bats. I hate bats. When I went in the back bedroom, I woke them up."

Lauren stared at Jac. "You're afraid of bats?"

"Hell, yeah."

"You know they won't hurt you, right?"

"You don't know that. They're icky, and they could get caught in my hair."

Lauren started to laugh. *Bats. She's afraid of bats.*

"It's not funny."

"It is. It really, really is. Afraid of a tiny little bat." Lauren bent double with laughter, and Jac swatted her butt.

"Hey, don't be laughing at the city girl. And it wasn't just one bat. They're hanging all over in there."

"Come on. Let's get you away from the terrifying creatures of the night."

Jac strode away, but glanced back over her shoulder. "They could be vampire bats, you know."

"We don't have vampire bats here. Our bats feed on insects, not people. Were they brown or grey?"

"Who the hell knows? I didn't hang around long enough to examine one."

"You know, they're probably hibernating in the attic. There must've been a hole in the second-floor roof they used to access the bedroom. You probably disturbed their sleep."

"Did you want me to write them an apology note?"

"I don't know. Do you speak bat?"

"I don't think you're being properly appreciative of the trauma I just suffered."

Lauren raised an eyebrow. "The trauma *you* suffered? I think you scared me out of seven years' growth with that scream. And by the way, it was a very girly scream."

"Was not."

"Was too."

Jac held out the newspaper. "Well, at least I didn't drop this." She nodded at the kettle in Lauren's hand. "Looks like you found a treasure too."

"I did. It probably hasn't moved in the last ten years." Lauren raised the kettle and peered at it. "I'm not sure it's salvageable, but I'd like to give it a try. It would be a real conversation starter."

"Not to mention a piece of your heritage. Your great-grandmother may have used that."

"That's a nice thought, isn't it?"

Jac nodded. "It is. And maybe you'll be able to hand it down to your granddaughter someday."

"I think you're missing a step there. I'd have to have kids first."

"I thought that was definitely in the plans. From the way your mother-in-law talked—"

Lauren sobered. "I'm not so sure anymore."

Jac stopped and studied her. "About having kids?"

"About...anything."

"Want to talk about it?"

Lauren started walking again. "Maybe." She was quiet for a few strides. "Last night, when Anjali was talking about Jeffrey..."

"She's crazy about him, isn't she? It's so obvious."

"She is. And he's the same way about her. They're best friends. They're never happier than when they're together, even if they're just at the Laundromat." Lauren sighed. "That's the way it should be, don't you think?"

"Mmm. Are you comparing your relationship with Phil to your sister's?"

"It's hard not to."

"Isn't Phil your best friend?"

"There was a time I thought so, but... Jac, is it different with women?"

"What do you mean?"

"Well, I have mostly female friends and a male fiancé. You have female friends and female lovers. Do you have difficulty at times differentiating between what you feel for someone? Is it more confusing because a woman has the potential to be either friend or lover?"

Jac didn't answer immediately. "I'm not sure I'm the best one to answer that. I think that the most wonderful relationship would be with a woman who is both my best friend and lover, but I've never had that kind."

"So you keep pretty clear boundaries between friends and lovers? The women you meet at Sous-terre fall on one side and, though I know it's not the best example since she's straight, Victoria falls on the other."

Jac blew out a breath of steam. "Actually..."

When she didn't go on, Lauren looked at her. "Actually what?"

Jac was silent.

"Jac? What's the matter?"

Jac looked to a grove of trees that lined the furrowed fields as a wind break. A large log lay on the ground. "Can we sit for a bit?"

"Sure." They scuffed through fallen leaves to the log and sat down. Lauren waited quietly while Jac collected her thoughts. *Something's really bothering her.*

"Vic and I...Vic... There's something you should know."

"Okay."

Jac hung her head and stared at the ground.

Lauren's eyebrows rose. "Oh my God...are you and Victoria lovers?"

Jac's head snapped up. "What makes you say that?"

"Because obviously something's upsetting you—something to do with Victoria."

"We were never lovers, but..."

Lauren waited. "But you wanted to be?" Comprehension dawned. "No... She wanted you, didn't she?"

Jac nodded.

"Before she got married?"

"After."

"Oh." Lauren blinked. "Oh." *Jesus.* "So she's... bisexual?"

"To my knowledge, she's never been with another woman."

Lauren nodded slowly. "So it was just you she wanted."

Jac sighed heavily. "I didn't encourage her, but maybe I didn't discourage her hard enough. She kind of got...obsessed. It was really bad for a while. She almost wrecked her marriage. Roger was sure she was having an affair, and I suppose emotionally she was, but we never slept together. Eventually, she got counselling, and he forgave her."

"I'm surprised you two are still able to be friends. I'm not sure I could in the same situation."

Jac flashed her a wry grin. "You mean if you were lusting after me and couldn't have me."

Lauren shifted uneasily on the log. "I mean, with all that unresolved tension. It has to be uncomfortable at times."

"At times, yes. For a while I cut way back on seeing her, but I missed my friend, and gradually we rebuilt our relationship on a safer plane."

"Huh. So the boundaries aren't always clear, then."

Jac shook her head and glanced at Lauren. "There's more."

"Okay." To Lauren's amazement, Jac's hands shook and she began to hyperventilate. "Hey, what's wrong? Jac?"

"I can't—I can't—"

What the hell's going on? Lauren slipped off the log and knelt in front of Jac. "Hey, it's okay. Whatever it is, it's okay." She was shocked to see tears in Jac's eyes so she pulled her into a hug and stroked her back. "Shhhh, whatever it is, don't worry about it. You don't have to tell me anything you don't want to. It really doesn't matter." She soothed Jac with hands and words until Jac stopped trembling.

They leaned on each other for long moments, until Jac pulled away and brushed her hand over her eyes. "I'm sorry. I don't know where that came from."

"Don't worry about it. What are friends for?"

Jac's eyes were red and the fine lines on her forehead were more pronounced, but she appeared to have regained control.

Lauren studied her. "You told me I could ask you anything. I just want you to know that you can tell me anything. No judgments, okay?"

Jac took a deep breath. "Okay."

Lauren rose to her feet and held out her hand. "Good. Let's walk a bit more and then head back to the house."

Jac took Lauren's hand and let herself be pulled up. "Sounds like a plan."

Chapter 13

Jac looked back over her shoulder as Lauren drove away from the farmhouse. *I hope I'll be back sometime.*

"I'm really glad you were able to come along," Lauren said. "It was a fun weekend, bats and all."

"Well, I could've done without the bats, but everything else was great. Your family is a lot of fun, and your farm is an oasis of peace in this crazy world."

"Thanks. I'll bring you up sometime this winter and take you skating at the creek. Sara would probably want to come along, if that's okay with you. Despite breaking her nose that one time, she loves to skate."

"Your sister is very sweet. I'd welcome her company. I guess Zac can't wheel out there?"

"Actually, Dad built a lift onto a small trailer that he pulls with his mini-John Deere, so he can take Zac out and about in the fields, even in the winter. When we were all going out to skate, Brian would drive the tractor with Zac loaded on the trailer. One time, Jason decided Zac had to go skating too. It took all of us to lower his wheelchair down the banks to the creek, but he had a blast zipping around the ice. We just about had to winch him back up, though, so he usually sat at the top and watched."

Jac imagined Zac whirling around the ice in his wheelchair, his head thrown back in laughter. *These are such good people.*

It was a much quieter trip home. Lauren appeared to be lost in thought, while Jac brooded over how to escape her predicament. It was only when they turned down the service road to Jac's place that she came out of her brown study.

A vintage cherry red 1965 Mustang sat in guest parking.

"Marc!" Jac sat up straight. "Oh my God, Marc's here."

Lauren glanced at her. "Your brother?"

"That's his car. I'd know it anywhere. It's just like him to show up on my doorstep without a word of warning. Oh, you have to come up and meet him."

Lauren wheeled her car in next to the Mustang. "I'd love to. But I can't stay long. It's time to face the music."

It took a moment for the words to sink in. "Face the music? What do you mean?"

"Well, in order of insult, I rejected the Carlton house, thus dissing Mrs. Emerson and her supremely good taste. I skipped out of the Marquettes' fabulous Fall Fling, no doubt ruining the beginning of the social season for Phil's entire family. And lastly, but not least, I went home and took you with me. That should be enough to start the festivities when I get back to the apartment."

Jac blinked, her joy dimmed by Lauren's sardonic recitation. "Are you sure you want to go home? You're welcome to stay with me for as long as you like."

"Thank you, but no. You've got company, and I have to talk to Phil at some point."

They walked to the entrance and Jac unlocked the door.

"Marc must have his own key, eh?"

Jac nodded. "He does. I gave him one after the time that he sat in his car all night waiting for me to get home because I was on a date and didn't know he was coming through town. Now he can come and go as he pleases, and I don't have to worry about him." She held the door for Lauren.

Jac's pace increased as she mounted the stairs. It had been months since she'd last seen her brother. By the time she got to her door, Lauren was half a stairway behind. Jac stopped and waited. "Sorry. I didn't mean to rush you."

A little out of breath, Lauren waved her off. "No worries. You're eager to see him. I understand."

Jac unlocked her door. Marc was coming down the hall toward her, a big grin on his bearded face. They came together in a fierce hug, and Marc whirled her in a circle.

When he set her free, she slapped his chest. "Why didn't you tell me you were coming?"

"I didn't know I was until yesterday. I've got a job interview in Fort Mac Tuesday morning, so I thought I'd stop and see my favourite sister on the way."

"I'm your only sister." Jac ruffled his beard. "This is new. What's with the mountain man look?"

"Don't you like it? I got bored with shaving this summer and decided to see how a beard would suit me."

"You look like a grizzly in the spring." Jac turned and tugged Lauren forward. "I want you to meet someone. Lauren, this is my baby brother, Marc. Marc, this is my dear friend, Lauren Blaine."

They shook hands. "Nice to meet you, Marc."

"You, too. I don't get to meet many of my sister's friends. It's a pleasure."

Jac beamed at them. "Why don't we go inside and have a drink?"

Lauren shook her head. "As much as I'd like to, I'd better go."

"Please? Just for a bit? I'd really like you two to get to know each other a little."

"Maybe…" Lauren glanced at her watch. "No, I'd better not."

Jac's shoulders slumped. "Okay. Next time, then. I'll walk you out."

Lauren said goodbye to Marc, who nodded and turned back to the living room.

Jac followed her out onto the landing. "Will you at least text me to let me know everything is okay? Please?"

"I'll try, but it might be a while." Lauren's brow was creased, and Jac wanted to smooth away the lines of tension in her face. "Have a good time with your brother, crazy red beard and all."

Jac cast a glance over her shoulder. "He does look pretty wild right now. He's actually pretty handsome under all that hair, if I do say so myself."

"So he looks like you, does he?"

Jac smiled. "He does, actually. And thank you."

"Just calling it like I see it." Lauren leaned in for a hug.

They lingered in the embrace, and Jac gave Lauren an extra squeeze before releasing her. "Remember I'm here for you, okay? If you need anything at all... In fact, wait a minute, all right?"

She went back into the apartment. "Marc, can I have your key to the place? I'll get you a new one before you leave."

"Sure." He pulled a key ring out of his pocket and worked a key off it.

"Thanks. I'll be right back." Jac hurried back to the landing and handed Lauren the key. "Here, take this. If you need some place to go or just to get away from...things, my home is yours to use any time...no notice needed."

Lauren stared at the key, then folded her fingers around it. "Thank you. I don't think I'll need it, but I appreciate the thought."

She turned to walk down the stairs, and Jac watched her go. *Please let her be all right.* Lauren waved before she disappeared from sight, but Jac waited until she heard the front door open and close before she returned to the loft.

Marc was sprawled on the couch, a beer bottle in his hand. He patted the couch. "I really like what you've done with the place. And this is going to be so much better than sleeping on the old one."

"It's great, isn't it? I owe it all to Lauren. She helped me pick out colours, do the painting, buy art, order new furniture, stain old furniture... She's an amazing woman."

"Remind me to thank her. Sleeping on that old couch was worse than going to see a proctologist."

Jac took a seat at the other end and studied him. "You're looking good, bro. Vancouver obviously agreed with you."

"It did, but you know me. Too long in one place and I start getting cabin fever. I got an offer from a buddy up north, so I thought I'd go check it out. It's a good chance to make some big bucks, at least for the winter, and if I like it, I'll hang around for a bit." He regarded her closely. "You're looking pretty good, yourself. What have you been up to lately?"

They spent some time catching up, and Jac told him all about her weekend at the Blaine farm.

He laughed when she came to the part about the bats. "You still get freaked out by those things? I'd have thought you'd grow out of that."

"Like you grew out of your commitment phobia?"

"It's not a phobia. It's just common sense. What woman is going to want to make a life with a rolling stone? You know I go crazy in one place too long, and it's not fair to make a commitment I know I can't keep."

"You have a point." Jac glanced at her phone. There was no message from Lauren yet. *Probably too soon. I'm sure she's fine.*

"Your friend seems nice."

"She's great. Meeting her was absolutely the best thing to happen to me in a long time."

"Yeah? So, is there something going on between you two?"

Jac shook her head. "No, she's straight…and engaged. Why do you ask?"

"Because that's the third time you've checked your phone in the last half hour. I've never seen you do that before, or have you become a slave to your electronics now, too?"

"No, I'm just a little worried about her."

"Why?"

"She's having problems with her fiancé, and I think she was heading home to have it out with him when she left."

Marc frowned. "Is he the type to get violent?"

"She says no, but I really don't like him." Jac shook her head. "Not that I made a good impression on him, either. It was mutual loathing at first sight."

"My big sister made a bad first impression? I find that hard to believe."

Jac glanced at her phone again. *Come on, come on.* "It happens. Phil knows I'm gay, and I think he views me as competition because Lauren and I get along so well."

Marc studied her for a long moment. "Are you?"

"Gay?"

He rolled his eyes. "Yeah, that's it."

"Ah, you mean, am I competition."

"Uh-huh."

Jac hung her head and didn't answer.

Marc finally poked her with his foot. "Hey, what's going on? Talk to me."

Jac closed her eyes. "I've fucked up so bad, Marc. And I have no idea how to fix things."

His foot rubbed against her leg. "Tell me. Maybe I can help."

"I doubt it." She took a deep breath, leaned back, and faced him. "I did a really dumb thing. A few weeks ago, Vic and I were at the bar. We ended up making a bet involving Lauren."

"A bet? What kind of a bet?"

"A horse's ass kind of bet, and I'm the ass who agreed to it. Vic bet me that I couldn't get a random woman she'd pick into bed within a month. She chose Lauren."

"Jesus. Did you even know her?"

"No."

Marc shook his head. "You befriended a straight chick just so you could sleep with her? That seems kind of callous."

"Callous, stupid, insensitive... Believe me, I've already called myself every name in the book. I'd give anything to go back and retract it."

"Then why don't you?"

"Because if I back out, I have to have sex with Victoria." Jac met Marc's gaze. "I really, really don't want to do that, for so many reasons."

"Huh." Marc toyed with his beer bottle.

"There's more."

"Seriously? What?"

"I...I've fallen for Lauren. I mean head over heels, ass over teakettle, way over the moon in love. It's insane. I've only known her three weeks, but I can't help it."

"Uh-oh. That complicates things."

"Ya think?" Jac laughed bitterly.

Marc leaned forward, rolling the bottle in his hands. "All right, let's look at things logically. You love Lauren, which I assume means you'd like to sleep with her."

"But not like this. Not because I made a stupid bet to do so."

"Well, there is that other thing, too. You said she is straight, and engaged. Would she even be interested in you that way?"

Jac shot Marc a shamefaced glance. "I've been seducing her for almost three weeks now. She's definitely interested, though I don't know if she's really aware of it. We slept in the same room last night—different beds—and I have to tell you, I'm almost a hundred percent sure that if I'd crossed the room and climbed into bed with her, she'd have welcomed me."

"Are you why she's having problems with her fiancé?"

"Probably. I mean, he's kind of a dick, anyway, but the time she's spent with me sure hasn't helped."

Marc scratched his beard. "Damn. How the hell did you get yourself into this mess?"

"Booze, boredom. There's really no excuse, and I know it. I just don't know how to get out of it."

"Okay, let's examine what you want out of the situation."

"That's easy. I don't want to sleep with Vic, but I also don't want to lose her friendship, which I will if I back out of the bet. I want to sleep with Lauren, but only when she wants to sleep with me and when she's free to do so. In the meantime, I don't want to lose her friendship. It's the best thing in my life. I can't imagine a day without her, even if we're just exchanging texts to say hi." Jac smiled and shook her head. "She drives this bright yellow VW bug, one of those that came with the vase of big white and yellow daisies on the dash. It's just so her. She's this incredible ray of sunshine. She's brought warmth and light and fun to my life."

"Wow, you've got it bad."

Jac sighed. "I do."

"When is the bet deadline?"

"Ten days from tomorrow. Time's running short."

"So your options are to sleep with Lauren to win the bet—"

"Which I don't want to do."

"I know. I'm just working things out in my head. Option two, admit defeat and sleep with Vic."

Jac shook her head.

"Option three, withdraw from the bet and maybe damage your friendship with Vic."

"I don't want that, either."

"There might be an option four."

Jac studied Marc. "What? Do you see a way out?"

"Maybe. Tell Lauren how you feel about her. If you're right, and she is interested in you—"

"She is."

Marc smiled. "I believe you. So, if she is, and she's in the process of breaking it off with Phil today—"

Jac glanced at her phone again. "I'm not a hundred percent sure that's what she's doing, though."

"But even if she's not, if you declare your love, you at least present her with options she might not think she has. Best-case scenario—you love her, she loves you, you both admit it and end up in bed together. You win the bet de facto. What were you supposed to win, anyway?"

"Aww, it's stupid."

"Yeah, well, tell me anyway," Marc said.

"Vic will try and convince her husband to go to Sous-terre." Jac shrugged. "Now that I think of it, that was also dumb to agree to. Whether Vic wins or loses, she probably thought it would end with us having sex. Whereas I was thinking that if they came to the club, I'd steer them to the couple's playroom without me. I just wanted to win the damned bet, no matter the stakes."

"You always were supercompetitive. I still remember the great marble fight between you and Leon when I was seven." Marc chuckled and finished his beer. "So just out of curiosity, would you ever take Lauren to the club?"

"If she wanted to go. She's asked me some questions about it, but I don't know if that means she's actually interested, or just curious."

Marc rose and went to the kitchen. "I think I need another beer. Want one?"

"Yes, please."

He returned and handed her a bottle before resuming his seat with his own beer. "It's kind of hard for me to square the way you described Lauren with someone who'd enjoy Sous-terre. I can't imagine your little ray of sunshine being into bondage."

"I wouldn't think so either, and I'd certainly never press her, but like I said, we've talked about it a few times, and she's been the one to initiate the conversation."

"It's probably just something that would never in a million years be part of her life, so she's flirting with the wild side."

"You're probably right." Jac sipped her beer, and the flavour reminded her of the chugging contest with Adam. She smiled. After the alcohol and presleep playfulness and conversation, it had required all her determination to resist crossing the small space between her and Lauren. It would've been so easy. She'd heard the arousal in Lauren's voice. It matched her own, but she was more adept at hiding it. *Good thing I can fake sleep with the best of them.*

She grimaced. She'd developed her faking skills during the times when she couldn't get out of staying with a woman, but didn't want to talk after sex. Many a conversation had been cut short when she shifted into her patented deep breathing mode.

"So have you decided what you're going to do?" Marc asked.

"Well, I'm not going to try to tell her about the bet again, that's for sure. I had a bloody panic attack when I tried to tell her this morning. I thought I was going to pass out."

"Seriously? You really thought you'd pass out?"

"Uh-huh. I couldn't catch my breath. I was so scared that she'd hate me and never want anything to do with me, I freaked out."

"What did she do?"

Jac closed her eyes, summoning the memory of Lauren's soft words and reassuring hands. "She was there for me. She must've thought I was crazy, but she couldn't have been kinder."

"She sounds like a keeper."

"She is." Jac sat up straight and looked at Marc. "I've made a decision."

He nodded.

"I'm backing out of the bet. I don't want to lose Vic's friendship, and I'll try hard to reason with her, but ultimately, keeping Lauren in my life is more important than anything else."

Marc smiled and leaned forward to touch his bottle against hers. "To Lauren."

"To Lauren." Jac tipped her beer back and took a swallow. Her phone vibrated, and she grabbed it.

All ok. Talk l8r. Miss U.

Relieved, she texted back, *Miss U 2. l8r.*

Marc snickered. "I wish you could see the goofy look on your face right now. You are so smitten."

Jac touched the screen where Lauren's words were illuminated. *He's right. I am.*

Chapter 14

Lauren sat on the closed commode, phone cradled in her hands. She read Jac's text, vision blurred by tears. *Everything is not okay, but if I tell you that, I know you'll want to rescue me. God, what do I do?*

She'd hadn't exactly taken refuge behind the bathroom's locked door, but Phil was far too angry to reason with, so she'd given herself a time-out.

Something else shattered in the living room, and she winced. She'd never seen Phil so furious and out of control. *Face it, you got pretty mad at him, too.* "Yeah, but I haven't broken anything." *Except maybe his heart.*

The apartment door slammed. Lauren waited and listened. When five minutes passed with no further sound from the other room, Lauren rose and opened the door a crack. Nothing.

She went to the living room. It was a mess. Couch cushions and dining room chairs were thrown about, her books were ripped and scattered on the floor, and the decorative mirror her parents had given them as an engagement gift lay in shards on the carpet. Several holes had been punched and kicked in the wall.

Lauren stared in shock, her heart pounding. Then she spun on her heel, went to the storage closet for her suitcases, and started gathering clothes and toiletries. Certain that anything she left behind would end up destroyed, she filled two suitcases with as much as they could hold.

Once packed, Lauren scanned the bedroom for anything she might've missed. There was nothing but a framed photo of her family, which she tucked into her purse. Then she took off her engagement ring and set it on Phil's bedside table.

She grabbed her coat and rolled her suitcases out to the elevator and down to her car. The VW listed at an odd angle. Her passenger side tires were flat. "What the hell!" She hurried around to check the other side of the car. Those tires were flat, too. Lauren knelt for a closer look; there were several gaping slashes in the sidewalls. She slammed her hand against the side of the car. *If he thought that was going to keep me here, he's insane.*

Lauren marched out of the garage, pulling the suitcases along behind her. She considered her options as she walked down the street. She thought of going to Jac's but knew there wouldn't be room for her with Marc visiting. Instead, she decided to get a room for the night and figure out her next step in the morning. She didn't want to stay too close to the apartment, so when she got in a taxi, she directed the driver to a place near a C-Train station. She would need transit to get to work the next morning.

Once she'd checked in, she stowed her bags and sat on the bed, head whirling. The urge to call Jac was overwhelming, but she fought it. Instead, she dialed her sister. When Anjali answered, Lauren started to cry.

"Laurie? What's wrong? What's the matter?"

"I think I just broke up with Phil."

"You think you did? Sweetie, what happened? And where are you?"

"At a hotel. We had a huge fight. He stormed out, and I packed up."

"Wow. Do you want to tell me what the fight was about?"

"Everything." *Jac, mostly.* "He's really upset with me for so many reasons that it's hard to pick one. I don't listen to him—or pay his mother proper respect. I'm never around anymore. I hang out with people he doesn't approve of." *Well, one person anyway.* "He feels that he gave up everything to be engaged and I haven't given up anything."

"Bullshit."

Lauren chuckled through her tears. "Trust you to be concise."

"I know you. I haven't met Phil, but I have to tell you, I do not like the way your world contracted when you guys got engaged. Seems to me you did all the bending and accommodating, and he went along on his merry way. No relationship can survive when it's one-sided."

Lauren contemplated Anjali's words. "Do you have friends you see without Jeffrey?"

"Of course."

"Really? Because you two are so close. You always seem happiest when you're together."

"We are, but we're not one person in two bodies. There's nothing I enjoy more than a rowdy girls' night out, and Jeffrey loves to hang with his old friends, too. We appreciate each other all the more when we're back home together again. And let me tell you, it makes for fabulous sex."

Lauren smiled and wiped her eyes. "TMI, sister of mine. So you don't think it was wrong of me to bring Jac home this weekend?"

"Hell, no. Why not bring a friend? Jac's a hoot, and you guys looked like you were having a great time together."

We always do. "I tried to present that logic to Phil, and he went ballistic."

"How ballistic?"

"On a scale of one to ten? About a twelve. Let's just say I'm glad I'm not going to have to clean up the apartment or worry about getting the damage deposit back."

"Damn, what's his problem? Is he really such a controlling son of a bitch? That's not good."

"I think he was just jealous."

"If your fiancé is jealous of time you spend with your family and friends, that's a red flag. I'm glad you broke up with him."

"Technically, we didn't say that to each other. When he stormed out of the apartment and I came out of the bathroom—"

"Were you hiding in there?" Anjali's voice sharpened. "Are you afraid of him?"

"I just thought we both needed time to cool off, and in a one-bedroom apartment, options are limited."

"You could've used the bedroom if he was in the living room."

Do I tell her? "The bathroom has the only door that locks."

"Jesus Christ! You were scared!"

Lauren shivered. "Maybe a little. But he didn't hit me or anything."

"I'm calling Adam, and we're coming down there right now."

"No. There's no need."

"Then I'm sending Jason. He's closer."

"No, really, I'm okay. Jason and Dad still have a lot of work to do before the snow comes. Please don't bother them." *And I don't want Mom to know...yet.*

"I'll bet Brian could be there in an hour and a half, the way he drives."

Lauren laughed. "You're going to volunteer Zac and his electric wheels next, aren't you?"

"I was working my way through the list."

"Seriously, I don't need anyone to rescue me, but I may need to call in a favour."

"Anything."

"Does your former roommate's mother still rent out her basement suite?"

"I don't know. I can ask. Do you want me to put you two in touch?"

"Yes, please. I'm okay at this hotel for a few days, but I want somewhere preferably furnished and close to public transit. It'll be bad enough paying for a cab tomorrow. Transit is way cheaper, and I sure won't be riding to work with Phil anymore."

"Back up. What do you mean paying for a cab tomorrow? What's wrong with your car?"

"Four flat tires."

"Fucking asshole! He flattened your tires?"

"I didn't see him do it, but they were fine when I parked after dropping Jac off. Then I went to leave after the fight and they were all slashed and flat as pancakes. I'm going to call the Auto Club to have it towed tomorrow, but until I get new tires, I'll use transit."

"Son of a fucking bitch. I should call the whole family, and we should march down there and teach him not to mess with our Laurie." Lauren's heart warmed at the indignation and protectiveness in Anjali's voice. "Are you okay for cash, sweetie?"

"I am. We'd been planning to merge our accounts but never got around to it, so it's not like he can clean me out, thank God. You know me—I'm a pretty good saver. I've got enough to get a new place...and four new tires."

"Okay, but you call me if you need anything... anything at all."

"Thanks. Anjali?"

"Yes?"

"Don't tell Mom and Dad yet, okay?"

"All right—just don't ask me not to tell Jeffrey, because I feel a rant coming on."

Lauren laughed. "Rant away. I'll probably do a little of that myself tonight."

But when they hung up, Lauren didn't feel like ranting. Exhaustion and depression settled over her, and she lay back on the bed. *How did this all happen? A few weeks ago, I was happily engaged.*

She snorted. "Get real. You weren't so much happy as complacent." *Then Jac came into my life.* "Did she ever."

She toyed with her phone and debated whether to text Jac with the latest developments. She sighed and set it aside. It wasn't really the kind of news you text. She decided to talk to Jac the next day.

Okay, no point in putting it off any longer. Jac picked up her phone and punched in a number. She breathed slowly, in an effort to calm her racing heart.

"Trevor Travel Agency. Victoria McDermott speaking."

"Hi, Vic."

"Oh, hi, Jac. What's up?"

"I have to talk to you. Could you meet me after work?"

"Sure. What time and where?"

"I'm going to be tied up here until about six. Can you meet me at the firehouse around then?"

"Okay. I have to work at our north end office this afternoon anyway, so it'll take me about that long to get there. See you then."

"Thanks. Um, Vic, is Lauren there?"

"No, she took today off. Said something about car troubles."

"All right, later." Jac hung up as Becca tapped on her door.

"Mr. Collier's here to see you."

"Thanks, Becca. Show him in."

Lauren flipped through a magazine in the waiting room at the tire shop, then set it aside and sighed.

"Long day?"

Lauren looked at the older gentleman who sat across from her. "You could say that."

He smiled. "It is Monday, but it's almost over and you can go home soon."

Home to a hotel room. Sounds positively alluring. Lauren nodded politely.

Her phone rang and she jumped, but it wasn't Phil's ringtone. She didn't recognize the number. "Hello?"

"Miss Blaine, it's Sandor Fregosian from the Fregosian Gallery?"

"Oh, hi, Mr. Fregosian. How are you today?"

"Fine, thank you. Miss Blaine, the tapestry you ordered was delivered this afternoon, so you may pick it up at your leisure. We're open until nine on weeknights and until five on Saturday."

"That's wonderful. I thought it would be at least next week before I heard from you."

"I did too, but the artisan had already planned another delivery for this week, so things fell into place."

"Great. I'll be by to pick it up. Thanks for calling."

"My pleasure."

Lauren ended the call, then began to text Jac, but stopped. *I think I'll pick it up and pop over to Jac's with it. If she and Marc haven't eaten yet, we can order pizza. Maybe I can get some time alone with Jac to talk.*

The thought of spilling the whole story to Jac lifted her spirits, which were severely dampened by a day of following housing leads after learning the basement suite was occupied. By the time the Auto Club had towed her car to the shop, she'd ended up last in line behind a long string of people swapping out summer tires for winters. So she'd taken transit to check out several possibilities and finally settled on one. It was a secondary suite over a garage, but fully furnished, with reasonable rent and good privacy. It came with a parking spot, and public transit was nearby. She'd put down first and last month's deposit and was set to take possession at the end of the week.

Lauren closed her eyes and let her thoughts drift. They revolved around Phil, her family, her new home—but mostly they circled back to Jac. She smiled at the thought of the declaration she'd drawn up and carried around in her purse for two weeks. She'd wanted to wait until they finished decorating, and the tapestry was the last piece she needed to complete the loft. She was eagerly anticipating Jac's laughter when she saw it.

"Mr. Harland, your car is ready." A technician hovered at the edge of the waiting area.

The older gentleman smiled and stood.

"Ms. Blaine, may I speak with you for a moment?"

"Yes?"

"We've encountered a problem." The technician sighed and took a seat beside Lauren. "Your car has been vandalized."

"I know. The four flats were a dead giveaway. That's why I had it towed in."

"It's not just your tires. Someone did a number on your engine."

"You've got to be kidding me."

"I wish I was." He glanced at the work order in his hand. "We put the new tires on and went to drive it out, and it wouldn't start. So we looked under the hood. Your distributor cap and spark plug wires have been yanked."

I'm going to kill him. "Can you fix it?"

"We can, but it's too late to get parts from the dealership today."

Lauren groaned. "What else can possibly go wrong?"

"Ma'am, we could probably give you a loaner. Depends whether it's been turned back in yet. Let me check, okay?"

"Thank you." Lauren drummed her fingers on her thigh. *Don't think about what Phil did. Think about seeing Jac and Marc, having some fun, eating some pizza, maybe a little private conversation with Jac...*

"Ms. Blaine?"

"Yes."

"The loaner is available. If you'll come with me, we'll fill out the paperwork."

"Thank you." Lauren followed the technician to the payment desk.

A few minutes later, she was on her way to the Fregosian Gallery in a black Ford sedan.

Jac pulled into her parking spot and saw Victoria waiting by the door. She tried to slow her heart rate. "Okay, just remember how you rehearsed it."

Victoria waved as Jac got out of her SUV.

They greeted each other with a hug.

Jac led the way inside. "I hope you haven't been waiting long."

"No, I just arrived a few seconds before you did. So did Marc leave yet?"

"Early this morning. His interview is tomorrow, and he wanted to get up there and settled in by tonight."

"I'm sorry I missed him."

Jac chuckled. "You should see him. He's got this wild Viking look going with a fluffy red beard and hair past his shoulders. I told him to go see a barber before his interview, but you know Marc."

Victoria followed Jac up the stairs. "Uh-huh. He'll listen to every word you say, and then do exactly what he wants."

"That's my baby brother."

They passed the second landing.

"So, what's the big mystery? What did you want to see me about?"

Jac took a deep breath. "I've been thinking a lot lately, and I want out of the bet. I want to call it off."

Victoria stopped at the third landing and glared at her. "What? Like hell. You don't get to back out just because you're going to lose."

Jac unlocked the door. "This isn't a game anymore. People are going to get hurt. I never should have agreed in the first place. It was a ridiculous bet, and I don't know what I was thinking when I agreed to it." She walked down the hall to the kitchen.

Victoria's voice rose. "You were thinking that you were God's gift to women, and you could fuck anyone you set your sights on. Don't blame me if Lauren proved too tough a challenge and failed to succumb to your charms. You've got one more week, and then you owe me. I am not letting you back out of this bet."

"What bet?" The icy voice came from above them.

Jac whirled to see Lauren standing halfway up the stairs. *Oh God, no!* Jac froze, her whole body numb.

"I said, what bet?" Lauren descended another step.

"Uh, we didn't know you were here." Victoria flushed and looked away.

Jac couldn't.

"Obviously. I was hanging the tapestry. You remember the tapestry, Jac? The one we picked out together? The perfect touch to finish our redecorating project? I was right. You'll like it. It looks brilliant over your bed."

Jac cringed at the anger in Lauren's voice.

"I believe there's a question on the floor, ladies. What bet?"

Jac sank down on the tall stool next to the kitchen island. "Tell her."

"Yes, do tell me, Victoria. What's this about a bet involving me succumbing to Jac's charms?"

Victoria cleared her throat several times. "Uh, well, it was just... Look, I mean, we'd been drinking at the time... We weren't, we didn't mean..."

Nausea rose in Jac's belly. "A few weeks ago, Victoria challenged me to bed the woman of her choice within one month."

"I see. And how did I become the lucky target?"

"Well, I thought you and Phil were real solid, so I didn't think Jac stood a chance with you."

"And what were the terms?"

As her world collapsed around her, Jac closed her eyes and longed desperately for the nightmare to end.

"If Jac won, Roger and I would go to this club she likes. And if I won, she'd go to the mountains for a weekend alone with me." Victoria's voice echoed as if from a great distance.

"I get the picture. And to win, Jac had to fuck me by when?"

Jac wrapped her arms around herself, her control crumbling. The anger and pain in Lauren's voice was agonizing. *God, why? Why did she have to be here? Why couldn't I have met her under honest circumstances? Why did I make that goddamned bet in the first place?*

"Next Wednesday. Lauren, I'm sorry. I really didn't think—"

"Didn't think what? That maybe she was better at the game than you figured? That maybe it might have some effect on my real relationship? That maybe, just maybe, you were ruining my life with your little wager?"

Lauren's voice cracked over them like a whip. "No, you two didn't think at all, did you?"

Lauren reached into her pocket as she descended the stairs. She tossed the spare key at Jac's feet. "I'll never need that again." She turned to Victoria. "Enjoy your weekend together. I hope you fuck each other's brains out." Spinning, Lauren hurried out.

Jac surged to her feet and ran after her. "Lauren, wait, please wait. I want to explain, I have to explain."

Lauren halted on the top step, but didn't turn around. "Explain what? That I don't mean any more to you than what's between my legs?"

Jac flinched at the rawness in her voice. "No. *No*, it's not like that. You have to believe me."

"I have to believe you? How could I ever believe you again? Everything you said, everything you did these last few weeks, all you wanted was to get me into bed to win some stupid bet. I thought we were friends. Jesus, I thought you were the best friend I'd ever had."

"We are friends. Lauren, when we made that bet, I hadn't met you. I had no way of knowing how close we'd get. I'd never have made that bet if I'd known you. I was trying to back out of it today."

Lauren stood trembling. "You know the irony?"

Her voice was so low that Jac had to strain to hear it.

"You didn't even have to work that hard. I was falling for you. No one has ever made me feel the way you did. God, I'm such an idiot."

"You're not an idiot. I'm the idiot, and I'm so sorry. Please forgive me. Give us a chance… Give *me* a chance. I'll make this up to you, I swear. Please, please don't go. However it all started, it brought us together. That can't be all bad, can it?"

Lauren turned slowly.

Jac held her breath.

Lauren's face was streaked with tears, and her lips quivered. "You just don't get it. It's not only that you made a fool of me, it's that you would treat any woman as nothing more than a blow-up doll for your amusement. I don't want to be around someone who has so little respect for herself and everyone else." She resumed her descent.

Jac fell to her knees on the landing. Each step Lauren took shattered another piece of her heart. She moaned and buried her head in her arms, rocking back and forth, fighting not to retch. Long after she heard the front door close, she dragged herself to her feet and returned to the loft.

Victoria was hunched over a half-empty glass, an open bottle of Scotch on the island in front of her.

"Want one?" Victoria pushed the bottle in Jac's direction.

Jac looked at the bottle distantly. "I think you should go."

Victoria nodded and downed the rest of her drink. "I'm so sorry. I never should have started this whole thing."

"We're equally culpable. In fact, there's more than enough guilt to go around."

"I still feel responsible. Look, why don't you let me talk to her?"

"No. Leave her alone. She doesn't deserve to be afflicted with the miserable likes of us. Just go."

Victoria nodded and brushed by.

Jac stared into space, her chest so tight she had difficulty breathing. "You won. I'll meet you at the cabin on Friday. I'll even bring the toy bag."

"Forget it. It's over."

"Over?" Bitterness and rage roared within, and bile rose in her throat. She longed to scream her pain until it drowned the mocking voice in her head. She hungered to smash everything in sight but couldn't bear to damage what Lauren had wrought. *What the hell's wrong with me? She's right. I'm an utterly contemptible piece of crap. What kind of loathsome, fucking monster does what I did?* Her lip curled, and she shook her head. "No, it's not. I pay my debts. You wanted this. Be there."

Victoria nodded hesitantly before hastening out the door and closing it behind her.

It was the perfect way to punish herself. Having sex with Vic all weekend rather than hanging out with Lauren would inflict the worst kind of pain on her heart. She took a perverse satisfaction in that. Lauren's parting words had flayed her soul, and she'd never forget them, or the woman who spoke them.

She turned to the island and dragged the bottle over. *One bottle won't be nearly enough.* She was about to tip it to her lips when a paper rolled and tied with a blue ribbon sitting on the counter caught her eye. She unrolled the parchment-coloured paper.

Bitter Fruit

Certificate of Achievement—Home Decorating

This is to certify that Jacqueline Lanier has earned her Beginner's Merit Badge in redecorating. The recipient demonstrated the highest levels of dedication, professionalism, and aptitude. She is hereby judged competent to undertake future projects under strict supervision.

Jac's tears fell thick and fast, but she strained to read the signature.

Lauren Blaine: Boss, Senior Architect, and Chief Decorator

"My God, what have I done? What have I done?"
Her head fell on crossed arms, the scroll clutched tightly in one hand, and she sobbed.

Chapter 15

"Mrs. McDermott on line one, Ms. Lanier."

"Thank you, Becca." Jac rubbed her eyes, gritty from lack of sleep, and picked up the phone. "Yeah, Vic?"

"Lauren didn't show up at work this morning."

Jac straightened as alarm flashed through her. "Did she call in?"

Victoria's voice was ragged. "No, no word at all. I called her home to see if she was on her way, and Phil said she doesn't live there anymore."

"What?"

"He was pretty nasty about it."

Jac stood and started to pace. "What exactly did he say?"

"I'm not sure I could repeat it all."

"Vic, what the hell did he say?"

"Among other things, he said she ran out on him Sunday night. Then he kind of laughed in a really scary way. You don't think he hurt her, do you?"

Jac froze. *God, no!* "Wait, you said Sunday night? Are you sure it was Sunday?"

"I wrote it down. Hey—we saw her last night, so she was okay."

"She wasn't okay. We saw to that." *Damn me to hell.*

"But she didn't say anything about leaving Phil."

Jac snorted. "Actually, she did. She said we ruined her relationship and her life."

"She did?" Victoria's voice was subdued. "I guess I sort of blanked out the details."

"Wish I could." Lauren's words were seared into her memory.

"What should I do? Do you think I should put in a missing person's report? She's never failed to call, even if she was just running late."

"She's never had her life ripped apart by experts before, either. I doubt the police would take a report yet, since she hasn't been missing even twenty-four hours. Do you have a number for her family?"

"No. I guess I could ask Phil—"

"I suspect he's not in a mood to cooperate." *Oh, Lauren, what happened? Why didn't you call me when you left him?* "I think we have to wait until at least this evening."

"Okay."

"Let me know right away if you hear from her."

"I will. Jac, are you okay?"

"Okay?" Jac closed her eyes. "No, I wouldn't say that I am."

"God, I'm sorry. I've been cursing myself ever since I left your place last night."

"Curse me. I'm the one who deserves it. I could've said no to that stupid bet. I'm an arrogant, insensitive bitch." *And I'm paying the piper now.*

"As you said, there's enough blame to go around. Please—let's forget about this weekend, okay? You don't have to go through with this."

Jac laughed bitterly. "You're wrong. I do."

Victoria was silent for a long moment. "All right. I'd better get back to work. Talk to you later."

"Later." Jac hung up and swiveled in her chair. *Where are you, love? Where did you go? Home? I hope so.* She pinched the bridge of her nose. It was a scythe through her soul to know that Lauren would've turned to her for comfort, before... *I'll bet that's why you came over. Not just to hang the tapestry. You wanted to talk to me, didn't you? You were looking for some reassurance, some support. God, I let you down so badly.*

Jac tried to return to work, but found herself staring at the numbers on her screen without taking any of them in. They didn't matter. Nothing mattered. *Where are you?*

An hour later, Victoria called again. "Lauren checked in with Irene."

"Thank God! Where is she?"

"I don't know. She said there was a family emergency, and she's taking a week of her vacation time. She's supposed to be back to work next Tuesday."

"Then she's probably gone home. Good. They'll look after her." Jac leaned back in her chair and gazed out the window. Not even the relief of hearing the news could penetrate her despair. Thanks for letting me know."

"You really care for her, don't you?"

"You have no idea."

"Are you sure about this weekend? It's all right to change your mind."

I made my bed, now I'm going to lie in it—literally. "Not going to happen. I'll meet you up there Friday evening after work."

"We could ride together if you want." Vic's words were hesitant.

"I'd rather not." *If this weekend ruins our friendship, too, I want to have a way to get home on my own.* "I'll meet you there about seven."

"Okay…and Jac, I know I said it before, but—I'm so very sorry."

"I know." Jac replaced the receiver and fought back the tears.

Victoria rose from her desk. "I'm going for lunch now, Irene. I'll be back by two. Can I bring anything for you?"

Irene didn't lift her eyes from her computer. "A turkey sandwich would be great, thanks."

"One turkey sandwich coming up." Victoria got her coat and left the office. She wasn't particularly hungry, hadn't been since the fiasco three days before, but since she'd promised Irene a sandwich, she headed for their favourite deli. Once there, she placed and paid for her order, and took a table to wait.

She fiddled with her phone. *Do I call her again? I don't care what she says. I know she doesn't want to be with me this weekend.* The previous day, she had tried again to let Jac off the hook, but Jac wouldn't allow it. *I've never heard her sound so hollow...so listless. She's scaring me.*

Her take-out order was placed in front of her. "Thank you." She glanced up and her mouth fell open.

Lauren regarded her coolly. "That seat taken?"

Victoria blinked and shook her head.

Lauren sat, arms folded across her chest, and studied Victoria.

"I...uh...didn't expect to see you."

Lauren snorted. "I guess you didn't."

"We were worried about you...I mean, when you didn't show up for work Tuesday morning."

"Who's we?"

Victoria flinched. "Me and Jac."

"That's hard to believe."

Victoria grimaced. "Look, what we did was terrible, but whether you believe it or not, we both care for you."

Lauren's eyes gleamed with unshed tears.

Victoria stared at the table. "Actually, Jac's very much in love with you."

"You don't know that."

"Yes, I do." Victoria raised her head and met Lauren's gaze. "I know you probably don't care and you have no reason to, but this is killing her."

"Did she call off her...rendezvous with you?"

"I've tried to call it off—repeatedly."

Lauren brushed at her eyes. "Then Jac's fine with paying up."

Victoria leaned forward and tapped the table. "If you think that, then you're crazier than we were. Jac's in hell. She's punishing herself, because the last thing in the world she wants to do is have sex with me."

"Punishing herself?"

"Yes. Trust me, it's not exactly good for my ego to admit that, but it's true. Jac would give her right arm not to have made that bet, and she'd give her left arm, too, if she could take back the pain she inflicted on you. I honestly think she feels that she owes it to you to sleep with me."

"What? That's bloody insane."

"Maybe, but Jac's in a really bad place right now. She's determined to punish herself for what she did to you."

Lauren scowled. "And sleeping with you is supposed to do that? If she's so keen on punishment, why doesn't she go to that damned club? I'm sure someone there would be happy to help her out."

Victoria studied her hands, unable to meet Lauren's gaze. "I don't know what I can say to convince you, but Jac is so deeply in love with you that I'm not sure she'll ever recover."

Lauren shook her head. "I don't know whether to believe you or not."

"It's not my intention to convince you. I'm just telling you the truth. You can do whatever the hell you want with it."

Lauren's arms unfolded, and she rested them on the table. "Will you tell me the truth?"

"I just did."

"No, not that. I want to know everything."

"Everything?" Victoria furrowed her brow. "What do you mean? Exactly what is it you want?"

"I want to understand how this happened. I was sailing along, living my life without a care in the world, and suddenly everything imploded. My fiancé went psycho. My engagement is over. My car was vandalized. I had to move to a new place. I lost my best—" Lauren choked back a sob.

Victoria looked up, and her eyes widened. "Oh, my God. You fell for her, too."

"Don't be ridiculous."

"Then tell me why you're here."

"I told you. I want to understand how this all happened. For God's sake, I was an innocent bystander."

Victoria shook her head. "No, there's more to it than that. You don't just want to understand how it happened. You want to understand how Jac could've done this to you."

Lauren sucked in a sharp breath.

Bingo. "Listen to me. If you believe nothing else, please know that all Jac wanted was to cancel our wager. She asked me twice, was asking me again on Monday, when..." She shook her head. "I wouldn't let her."

"Why? Why wouldn't you let her out of it? What did I ever do to you?"

Victoria closed her eyes for an instant. "You probably won't believe this, but it actually had nothing to do with you, except that on the spur of the moment I needed what I thought was an impossible target. I never in a million years thought you'd fall for her."

"Okay, so maybe it makes sense, in a weird and warped kind of way, why you dragged me into this, but why even challenge Jac like that? How did you know she'd agree to something so...so..."

"Repugnant?"

"Cruel. I just can't square the Jac I know with a woman who would treat other women so cavalierly."

"I doubt it ever crossed Jac's mind to think of it that way."

Lauren scowled. "You're kidding. How could it not?"

"Because it was a seduction. Until you said yes—until you wanted to sleep with her too—she wouldn't have pressured you. In her mind, it's essential to give pleasure and get pleasure in equal measure. It's what she does, and she's very good at it. I thought you'd be invulnerable, but I didn't bank on the instant and unbelievable chemistry between the two of you." Victoria rolled her eyes. "You were straight and engaged and honourable to a fault. How much safer could you be?"

"I'm not sure if I should be flattered or insulted."

"You should be angry. I'm so angry at myself that I can't begin to tell you."

Lauren shook her head. "I don't get it. I don't understand how you can be happily married—at least you always talk about Roger like you two are happy—and still want to sleep with Jac. What is your obsession with her?"

Victoria flushed. "She told you, didn't she?"

"A little. I know you once almost wrecked your marriage over her. So why are you taking this chance again? Why did you go to such extremes when the risk is so high if Roger finds out? Are you in love with her?"

"You may not believe this—"

"You've been saying that a lot."

"I know, but sometimes I find it unbelievable, too. I'm actually very much in love with my husband. I don't want to leave him for Jac. I just—I'm not even sure I can explain it. My therapist had some fancy psychobabble term for it, but basically he meant I'd fixated sexually on Jac. He was right, but I thought we'd worked on it enough that it wasn't a problem anymore."

"And now? You're obviously still fixated on her or you wouldn't have made the bet."

Victoria folded trembling hands together. "I guess I thought if I could just—"

"Have an affair with her?"

"Not even an affair. One night together—one time together, and maybe I could get her out of my system." Victoria grimaced. "She's so damned—"

"Sexy."

"More than that. Hauntingly erotic. Knowing she goes to that club, what she does there…"

"She told you?"

"Not in a lot of detail, but enough that I can't resist filling in the blanks, and it drives me crazy. I wanted to win the bet, but even if I lost, at least I'd have gotten to see her in action."

"With your husband at your side." Lauren's tone was desert dry.

Victoria mustered a chuckle. "You have a point. Roger would definitely not approve of me playing with Jac at Sous-terre, whether he was there or not."

"Does he know you're meeting her this weekend at the cabin?"

"I told him I was going to the cabin, but not why or who with. He's going to be out of town anyway, and it's not unusual for me to go up there solo."

"So you are going to follow through? You're going to meet Jac tomorrow?"

Victoria couldn't meet Lauren's gaze. "It's what she wants."

"You told me it really wasn't."

Victoria's shoulders slumped. "You're right. It's the last thing she wants." Weariness settled over her. *Time to go back to Dr. Eichler. He's going to have a field day with this mess.*

"Then why are you making your best friend do something she'll hate doing? Shouldn't you be looking out for her? Stop her from making such a mistake?"

"She's an adult. She has the right to make her choices." As wrong as Victoria knew it was, part of her still hungered for Jac.

"Even when they're bad decisions? And ones you could prevent?"

Victoria's eyes filled with tears. "I don't know what to do."

"I do, but I need some more information."

Chapter 16

JAC WAS RAW. HER HEART, her head, her body—they all felt as if they'd been flayed from within. She'd had so little sleep that week that she knew she wasn't safe to drive, but she didn't care. If she got in an accident, it would be just payback for the pain she'd inflicted on Lauren.

She negotiated another hairpin curve. The old logging road that led to Victoria's family cabin was tricky to navigate, particularly in the gathering dusk. It sliced through thick, old-growth forests as it wound its way up the side of the mountain. Small waterfalls tumbled down steep rock faces to the left, and towering pines rose from the crags below to the right. There was no room for error or woolgathering. Jac had been there several times with Victoria and Roger, but still had nearly missed the turn-off from the main road.

Should have kept going. She lifted a hand to her temple and massaged deeply, trying to ease the headache that had barely let up since Monday.

Jac longed for Sunday night and a respite from this nightmare. Maybe it was time to use some of the backlog of vacation time she'd accumulated in her workaholic years. She could easily become a hermit for a month. It wasn't as if anyone would miss her.

The thought of hiding completely away from the world appealed to her. Nothing else had since Lauren walked out her door—not food, not sleep, not sex.

She groaned. "Definitely not sex. Why the hell didn't I accept Vic's offer and stay home tonight?" Perversely, her abhorrence of what awaited in Victoria's cabin kept her foot on the gas and her hands steady on the wheel. "Fucking serves me right." Tears filled her eyes, and she angrily dashed them away. She didn't deserve even the small comfort of a good cry.

Jac spotted the clearing ahead that signaled the approach to the cabin and downshifted. She swerved to avoid the huge pothole that Victoria's father swore to fill in every spring. She turned up the short access road and came to a bumpy halt when her headlights illuminated the front of the log structure. Despite her depression, she took a moment to appreciate the view.

Victoria's great-grandfather was a logger, who had originally built the cabin to house his family. Over the decades, successive generations had maintained the small building as a vacation home, and when additions were built, they were carefully wrought to be in keeping with the pioneer structure. Nestled under pines, the cabin blended with its environment. It appeared to have grown with the forest rather than as an incursion of man. A visitor could stand on the porch, look out over the valley, and listen to the roar of the glacier-fed river that provided water to the cabin.

Bitter Fruit

There was a trail of smoke from the large stone chimney, though no light shone in the windows. Victoria's car wasn't there. *Vic must have been here already and lit a fire. She's probably at her aunt's place waiting for the chill to come off.*

There were only a handful of homes along the old road. Victoria's aunt and uncle were among those who had a grandfather clause that protected their residence when the government declared the area free from development.

Jac walked around her vehicle and unlocked the back gate. She'd seen many patches of fresh snow on the drive up. *I hope Vic built the fire high.* She took out a small duffel bag, her thick, fleece-lined barn coat, and a leather satchel, slammed the door closed, and hurried to the cabin. She sighed in relief as the doorknob turned easily. *Good thing she left it unlocked.*

Jac stepped inside, instantly grateful for the warmth. Despite the fire blazing in the hearth of the great room, without the electric lights, the dim interior was only faintly illuminated. Jac dropped her bags by the door and started toward the fireplace.

A silent figure watched her from the old rocking chair next to the fire.

Jac's knees buckled, and she grabbed the back of the couch. "Lauren?"

The silence was broken only by the crackling of wood and the snapping of the flames.

Finally, Lauren nodded at the armchair opposite her. "Looks like you'd better sit down before you fall down."

Jac stumbled around the end of the sofa and dropped into the armchair, her gaze fixed on Lauren. She tried to speak, but couldn't form any words. A smile flickered over Lauren's lips, and she took a sip from her wine glass.

Jac was entranced by the firelight dancing across Lauren's face and the ruby depths of the wine. *Am I dreaming?* A surreptitious pinch convinced her that Lauren was really there.

She wore a formfitting black turtleneck tucked into faded jeans. The sleeves were pulled up to expose her forearms, and her legs extended in front of her, hiking boots crossed comfortably at the ankles. She was the picture of relaxation. Her shadowed eyes were serious, but there was no trace of anger in them.

A rush of hope swept through Jac. *Has she forgiven me? Do we have a chance?*

Lauren's impassive expression gave nothing away.

"Um, I thought. I mean... Where's Vic?"

"Victoria and I had a long talk yesterday. We agreed it would be better for all concerned if I met you here tonight. She brought me up here earlier and left hours ago." Lauren's tone was cool.

Jac didn't know what to think. She didn't want to make a single false step and ruin what might be a second chance. *It has to be a second chance, doesn't it? She wouldn't be here otherwise, would she?* She nodded at the wine glass Lauren held. "May I have a glass?"

"No."

Jac blinked.

Lauren gave a little sigh, set her glass on the side table beside the wine bottle and leaned forward. "I've done a lot of thinking since Monday night. In fact, that's about all I've done."

Unable to meet her gaze, Jac dropped her head. "I didn't mean to make you end your engagement. I'm sorry—" She stopped abruptly. *Why am I saying that? Don't lie to her. I'm not sorry. I've wished Phil to the other end of the earth a thousand times.*

Lauren shook her head. "I told you once that no one makes me do anything I don't want to. All you and your little scheme did was crystallize problems I'd been ignoring. For all your callous disregard of my feelings, the simple fact is that if Phil had been the right one for me, nothing you did could've broken us up."

Jac flinched. *Can't argue with that.* "How did Phil take it?"

"How do you think he took it? Badly, to say the least."

Jac's head snapped up, and she glowered.

"He had the right. I hurt him, almost as badly as you hurt me. He hasn't been at his best lately, but he's basically a good guy, and he did love me in his own way. He can't believe that his world and his future fell apart so quickly. I think it will take him a long time to get over this."

Lauren leaned back in the chair and began to rock. "I went home for a couple of days. After a lot of thinking, walking, and talking to my mom, I came back to the city. I went looking for Victoria yesterday, and we had a long talk. So here I am."

There was no enthusiasm in Lauren's voice, no joy or anticipation at the prospect of being there, and Jac still wasn't sure what it all meant.

With a smile that didn't reach her eyes, Lauren picked up her wine and took another sip. "Okay, this is the way it is. You have a choice, Jac. We can leave here together tonight, and when we get back to town, maybe we can be friends again. It would take time and work, and I'm not even sure if we can repair the damage, but I'm willing to give it a try. However, if we leave tonight, that's *all* we'll ever be—friends."

Jac held her breath.

"Or we can stay the weekend on *my* terms, and maybe when we leave on Sunday, we'll have a chance for much more than friendship. The choice is yours. You're obviously not averse to wagering. Are you willing to bet on us, on giving our relationship a chance?"

Jac's heart soared. *A chance? We have a chance?* She could hardly believe her ears. Then her mind processed what Lauren said. "On your terms? May I ask what those terms are?"

For the first time, a genuine smile appeared on Lauren's face. "Bring your bags over here."

What on earth is she up to? Jac retrieved her bags from the doorway and set them down by her own chair.

Lauren gestured. "Over here."

Jac picked up the bags and set them beside Lauren. She hesitated, hoping for an invitation to stay.

Lauren shook her head, and Jac retreated to her chair.

"Victoria and I had a long and interesting talk. She clarified some things for me…things I've been thinking about a lot. I think I understand you better now. I even have a clearer idea of why you agreed to the wager in the first place."

Jac dropped her gaze.

"You know what puzzled me for the last few days?" Jac shook her head.

"I couldn't reconcile the sweet, considerate, funny, lovable woman I'd gotten to know with a sexual predator who would target someone without regard to the effect her actions would have. Over and over, I examined every second we spent together. I asked myself if you were some kind of sociopath, or if you were that good an actor that you could've pulled this off. I questioned how I could have been so dumb, so gullible, and naïve."

Even though Lauren's voice held no anger, Jac's heart sank. She stared at the toes of her boots.

"Finally, I came to a conclusion: I wasn't that dumb, and you weren't that good an actor. However it started, what happened between us was real."

Jac's head snapped up. "Yes. It was."

Lauren nodded. "I know, and in an odd way, you were right about it being a good thing that asinine wager brought us together."

Jac hesitated. "I'm not sure what to say. I'm profoundly glad that we met. It was like being torn in half when you left Monday night, but if I could spare you the pain and humiliation my actions have caused you, I would. I'm so very sorry for hurting you."

"I know you are." Lauren sighed. "My mom has a saying. If you sow an onion seed, you won't harvest a peach."

"I'm sorry?"

"Yeah, I don't know where she came up with it either, but it basically means if you sow something bitter, you're not going to reap something sweet."

Jac's throat tightened, and she fought to hold back the tears. "And because our relationship started with something as nasty as that damned wager—"

"Exactly. How could anything good possibly come out of that?"

Jac looked away, unable to meet Lauren's gaze.

"Which brings us back to my terms for the weekend. My conversation with Victoria was very enlightening. She told me some things about your exploits at Sous-terre."

Jac gulped. *Oh God.* Her gaze flicked to the satchel beside Lauren's chair.

Lauren reached over and dragged the satchel in front of her.

Jac slumped in her chair and covered her eyes.

Lauren chuckled.

Jac peered through parted fingers.

Lauren examined the contents. "Do you need these things?"

"Need?"

"Yes, do you *need* them? You never really made that clear when we talked about your after-hours exploits, and it seems like a simple question."

Jac considered her answer. "I don't need them. I mean they're just toys to increase the pleasure for myself and my partner."

Lauren touched something inside the bag. "Pleasure? This looks like it'd be more pain than pleasure."

"The two are often intertwined."

"Mmm." Lauren closed the satchel and slid it out of the way. "Here's what I've been thinking. What you've been about, what the damnable bet was all about, is power and control. For whatever reason, it's been your driving force. Would you agree?"

Jac squirmed. "Yes, but that's not what we were about."

"My point exactly. I certainly don't have your sexual expertise, and Phil was...well, he was pretty conservative when it came to sex, but I've done a lot of reading and research and thinking. I'm not averse to trying things outside my realm of experience, but if we're going to have a serious relationship, then it has to be one based on equality. The problem is, I'm not sure you can give up total control, and I won't accept anything less than a true partnership."

Jac mulled over Lauren's words as she analyzed past relationships, both casual and serious. It was true that she always held the balance of power. Whether in romance, friendships, or even business, every relationship was conducted on her terms, up to and including when it ended. She had never allowed herself to be vulnerable to anyone, ever. *Can I change? Do I want to?*

Jac met Lauren's gaze. *Yes, for her I can.* "What did you have in mind?"

Lauren smiled. "I don't want or need you to alter the essence of who you are. But I need you to trust me and I need to trust you, especially after what's happened between us. Monday night...I've never felt pain like that before. I can't even begin to describe it."

Jac closed her eyes, tears welling over. "You don't have to. I...I couldn't describe the pain of watching you walk out of my life, either."

"I pray we never hurt each other that way again. I don't think I could take it." Lauren's voice trembled.

Jac wiped her eyes. *I don't think I could either.* "What do you need from me?"

Lauren rocked slowly. "To demonstrate that you have the capacity to grow into this relationship, because I don't intend to take us lightly. If you agree, if you want to explore fully whatever this is between us, I need to know you'll dedicate yourself to nurturing it as completely as I will. If you can't give an honest commitment to that, then we should leave now."

Be sure. Be absolutely sure. You can't screw this up again. She deserves better. Finally, Jac nodded. "You have my heart, Lauren. You have my unconditional commitment to *us*."

"All right, then for this weekend, you're mine. I get to call the shots until we leave on Sunday."

Jac's eyes widened. "You're going to top me?"

Lauren chuckled. "I was thinking of it more as a couple's retreat and trust-building exercise, but you can call it whatever you like. Last chance to back out. Are you ready to gamble on us?"

Jac swallowed hard. *God give me strength.* She had a feeling that Lauren was going to put her through the wringer, at least psychologically. "Yes."

"Good. It was a long drive up here. Why don't you use the washroom, and then grab a couple of pillows and bring them back here."

Without a word, Jac went to the larger of the two back bedrooms and took two pillows from the bed. *I wonder if we'll end up in here together at some point. Don't know that I'd bet on it.*

After dropping the pillows on the couch, she made use of the washroom. As she washed her hands, Jac stared into the moonlit mirror. "What are you getting yourself into?" *This is Lauren, you twit. What the hell are you afraid of?* She dried her hands and hung the towel, taking her time. *I'm afraid I'll let her down, again.*

With a final glance in the mirror, Jac stiffened her shoulders, took a couple of deep breaths, and returned to Lauren, who smiled and lifted her wine glass in an unspoken toast. "Take off everything except your pants."

Jac swallowed hard, but began to unbutton her denim shirt. Her trembling fingers fumbled with the buttons, and she cursed her lack of coordination. *God. You'd think I was a thirty-year-old virgin on her wedding night.*

Cool hands closed over hers, stilling their tremors.

"I won't hurt you. I would never hurt you." Lauren's voice was gentle and reassuring.

Jac met her gaze and nodded. "I know." *I know you'll take far better care of my heart than I've taken of yours, but I swear things are going to change.*

Lauren laced her fingers behind Jac's neck and pulled her into a long kiss.

Jac lost herself in sensation, until Lauren pulled away.

"Finish up. I'll put some more wood on the fire. I don't want you to get cold."

Cold? She has to be kidding. I'm on fire here. Jac finished undoing her buttons as Lauren piled two more logs on the healthy blaze. After stripping off her shirt and bra, she sat down to untie her boots.

Lauren dropped a pillow midway between their chairs, then settled back in her rocker and waited while Jac kicked off her boots and thick wool socks.

When she was down to her jeans, Lauren nodded at the pillow. "Kneel there."

Jac sat back on her heels and knelt. She placed her hands on her thighs and held her shoulders and spine stiff.

Lauren's gaze drifted lazily over her half-naked body. She refilled her glass. Jac's breath caught. Without even touching her, Lauren had aroused her to unexpected levels.

Lauren took a sip of her wine and grinned. "At least I'm in no danger of drowning this time."

"You knew?"

"Not at the time. But after everything that happened this week, I figured out that you were putting on a show in the shower."

Jac gave a sheepish smile. "I was just removing the paint."

"Sure you were. Odd how you spent such a long time scrubbing areas that the paint never touched."

"Um, cleanliness is next to godliness?"

Lauren laughed, and then fell silent. Her gaze traced Jac's curves, and her hand trembled.

Jac submitted to the erotic survey, even as her body demanded attention.

Lauren rose and stood in front of Jac. "Up straight."

Jac straightened and faced Lauren's chest, which rose and fell with her rapid breathing. *I'm not the only one affected. Thank God.*

Lauren sank to her knees, still holding the glass of wine. She offered Jac a drink.

Jac rolled a sip on her tongue, surprised to find it was her favourite French red. After a couple more swallows, Lauren took the glass away and Jac ran her tongue over her lips.

"Put your hands behind your back and don't move. Don't touch me, and don't touch yourself."

Jac nodded.

Lauren dipped her finger in the wine and traced it over Jac's collarbone. Her warm tongue followed the same path. Jac quivered as Lauren trailed the wine down between her breasts and around the soft curves. She clutched her wrist so her hands wouldn't fly forward and seize Lauren's head as her tongue tantalized. *God, she's going to kill me.*

Her breath grew ragged as Lauren painted her taut nipples red and laved them clean. Jac feared her heart might burst from her chest as Lauren explored her body: thoroughly, sensually, slowly. She fought the urge to pull Lauren into her arms and rip her clothes off. It took every ounce of her will, but she submitted.

When Lauren pulled away and the teasing strokes stopped, Jac bit off a plea for more. Chest heaving, she waited.

Lauren set her empty glass aside, reached for Jac's waist, and undid the buttons of her jeans.

Jac wasn't prepared for the peal of laughter as Lauren slid her pants down to her thighs. Startled, she looked down.

"Dilbert? You're wearing Dilbert underwear? Why do I get the impression your heart wasn't really in this weekend?"

"Because it wasn't? At least not when I dressed to come up here."

Lauren's mirth showed no signs of subsiding.

"Hey, do I laugh at your underwear?"

"Darling, I promise you, I am *not* wearing Dilbert shorts." Lauren pulled Jac's jeans and underwear down to her knees.

Jac wavered. "Oh God, Lauren. What are you doing to me?"

"Teasing you. Teaching you. Loving you." Lauren picked up her empty glass and returned to her rocker. She poured another glass as she studied Jac.

Jac had never felt so exposed, or so excited. Always alpha in sexual games, she prided herself on her control, but she was a hair's breadth away from losing it. *Look at her. She's looking at me like a lion watches its prey.*

Lauren's hungry gaze swept over her body and stilled when it reached the red triangle between her legs. Lauren's nostrils flared, and Jac wondered if the scent of her desire was detectable.

Helpless to stop the trembling that shook her body, Jac could only plead with her eyes. She ached for Lauren's touch—needed it as desperately as the air she breathed.

Lauren set her glass aside and reached for the button of her own fly.

Jac's gaze followed her fingers as she slid the zipper down. She caught her breath when Lauren slipped a hand under the waistband of dark silk panties. Jac breathed in time with the rise and fall of Lauren's hand. *Oh God…please…*

She was paralyzed, except for the quivers that started from her clit and fluttered through her whole body. She listened raptly to the deepening of Lauren's breathing, and her body jerked sympathetically when Lauren uttered a small cry and stiffened.

Lauren extracted her hand, fastened her pants, closed her eyes, and rocked slowly.

Jac closed her eyes, tried to calm her breathing, and focused on delaying her own gratification. She was so intent on her task that she didn't notice Lauren move until she stood in front of her. Lauren traced her lips, and Jac eagerly took her fingers into her mouth.

Lauren dropped her other hand on Jac's head, caressing and soothing.

Jac whimpered when Lauren extracted her fingers.

"Shhh. You're all right. Let's get those jeans off you."

Jac sat on the floor and hastily pushed her pants and shorts over bare feet. Desire made her clumsy, and she wavered as she resumed her kneeling position.

Lauren firmly pressed Jac's shoulders down until her head rested on her arms against the other pillow.

"Please, oh please." Jac parted her thighs.

Lauren dropped to her knees and glided gentle hands over Jac's back. "You are so beautiful. It was the first thing I noticed about you—how you turned the head of everyone in the restaurant. I didn't understand my feelings that day. I'd never reacted to anyone, man or woman, like that before. But you, you haunted me from that very first meeting."

Lauren caressed Jac's ass, and her hips began to rock. "After we went to the concert and I discovered how much I liked the woman inside that gorgeous exterior, I couldn't stop thinking about you."

Lauren's hand trembled as it drifted up the delicate skin of Jac's inner thigh while the other ran underneath, over her abdomen, to cup and tease a rigid nipple before sliding over to its mate and inflicting the same delicious torture.

Jac stifled a moan. *Patience—patience—patience.*

Her mantra didn't slow the arousal that curled in her belly. Her body was so sensitized that she felt the shadow of Lauren's path over her flesh as acutely as the hands that drove her desire to new and powerful heights. Distracted by the multitude of sensations assailing mind and body, Jac uttered a tiny scream when Lauren penetrated her, sliding smoothly inside. Frantically, she thrust back. "More. Please, more."

Lauren hesitated for a moment, then obliged, filling and stretching her with a second finger.

Absorbed in the pleasure of being taken, Jac barely noticed when the hand that had been caressing her breasts traveled down her belly and came to rest between her legs. But when a delicate touch stroked her swollen clit, she sobbed in relief.

"You're safe. It's okay to let go. Trust me." Lauren's whispers filled Jac's ears.

Jac's body jerked frantically, as she sought absolution in the inexorable hands and heart that possessed her, drove her, and released her. With a loud cry, she climaxed and shuddered as Lauren gentled her back to sanity with soft words and soothing touches.

Jac fell forward as aftershocks rocked her body.

Lauren rolled her over and took her into an embrace.

Jac clung to Lauren, resting her head on a soft breast. It was only when Lauren's fingers brushed at her cheeks that she realized she was crying. "I love you, I love you, I love you."

"And I love you, my beautiful one. Rest now. I'm not going anywhere."

With that assurance, Jac let lassitude take her, completely content to be sheltered in Lauren's arms. When Jac awoke, the fire had burned low. She raised her head to meet Lauren's gaze. "What have you done to me?"

Lauren smiled. "Only what I intend you to do to me soon."

Jac's breath caught. She wasn't sure about the rules of this game they were playing, but she was determined to stick to Lauren's directives. "Soon? As in, tonight? I get to make love to you, too?"

Lauren eased out from under Jac's body and stood.

Jac watched, quivering, as Lauren stripped off her clothes and boots.

When Lauren stood naked in front of her, she extended a hand. Jac took it and rose to her feet.

Lauren moved into her arms, and they clung to each other. Finally, Lauren drew back. She held Jac's hands and gazed at her. "I love you, Jac. There can be no more deceit between us…ever."

"I love you, too. I'll swear I'll never fail you again."

Their bodies surged together, and Jac brought her mouth down on Lauren's. She revelled in the sensation of Lauren's kisses, running her hands over Lauren's back and down to cup smooth, firm cheeks.

Flushed, Lauren pulled back. "Bedroom. Now."

Jac led the way. With a little grin, she glanced over her shoulder. "Are you going to let me put clothes on at all this weekend?"

"Oh, I'll let you put on boots if we go for a walk tomorrow. Wouldn't want you out of action because of frozen toes."

"What about other frozen bits and pieces?"

"Not to worry. I'll keep everything else warm."

A grin crossed Jac's face before another thought occurred to her. "Hey, does this mean I still owe Victoria a sex weekend?"

That earned her a sharp smack to her buttocks, and she yelped. "I take it that means no." She laughed as she turned around and backed up in front of Lauren, rubbing her ass as she did. "Damn, woman, that's quite a hand you have on you."

"Oh, for heaven's sake. Compared to what you have in that bag, I'm surprised you even felt it." Lauren stopped. "In fact, go get the toy bag."

Jac made an elaborate, sweeping bow. "Your wish is my command."

"It is this weekend."

Jac scampered back to the rocker to grab the satchel. *What have I gotten myself into?* With a huge grin, she shook her head. *Don't know. Don't care.*

She double-timed it back to the bedroom.

Chapter 17

Lauren woke first. The bedroom was filled with grey light and sleet pelted against the windows. *What a perfect day to stay near the fireplace…or in bed.* Jac's breathing tickled the back of her neck and one arm was slung over her, hand resting limply against the sheet. Lauren felt a fleeting pang as she eyed the chafe marks on Jac's wrists. *I should've loosened them sooner.*

They'd been working their way through the toy bag. Jac was a delectable sight with her wrists cuffed to the iron rails of the headboard and ankles tied to the base rail. Lauren had taken time to delight in Jac's responses as she experimented and mapped her lover's body. But Jac's inability to stay still under her ministrations had caused her to pull sharply against her restraints, digging them into her wrists and ankles. *Not that she seemed to mind the end results.*

She gazed at the window, and a flash of doubt niggled within. By most measures, the night has gone well. She'd been elated at how readily Jac yielded control and how sincere her desire was to let Lauren set their course. Jac hadn't even seemed to notice her lover's moments of awkwardness and uncertainty.

She smiled. *All that research and fantasizing paid off. I don't think Jac had any idea of how nervous I was.* Her smile faded and she took a deep breath. *I think we're going to be okay. I've never in my life felt more loved. I hope she feels the same.*

A thrill ran through her as she sifted through memories of their lovemaking. *We're both going to be exhausted by the time we go home tomorrow. Glad I don't have to go in to work until Tuesday. I wonder if I can talk Jac into taking Monday off, too.*

Lauren rolled over, and Jac mumbled as she adjusted to her bedmate's new position, though she didn't wake up. *Poor thing. I think I wore her out. But I suspect she'll be happy to return the favour…if I let her.*

She studied Jac's features, which were soft and relaxed in slumber. *Thank God she agreed to my terms. I don't know what I'd have done if she hadn't. I can't even imagine my life without her.* Her heart ached at how close they'd come to throwing their love away. *What if Victoria hadn't agreed? What if Jac was waking up with her this morning?* A sudden need to see her eyes led Lauren to brush her fingers down the side of Jac's face and over her lips.

Jac's eyelids fluttered and opened. "Good morning, sweetheart."

"Good morning, love."

Jac smiled and pulled Lauren closer. "What were you thinking so hard about?"

"How do you know I was?"

"Because you get a tiny line here when you're thinking deep thoughts." Jac touched the space between Lauren's eyebrows.

"I do, do I?"

"Mmm-hmm." Jac rolled on her back and stretched. She lifted an arm in invitation and Lauren snuggled into her. "How are you feeling this morning?"

Lauren rose up on an elbow. "A little sore, but wonderful. What about you?"

"I don't think I've ever felt better." Jac's gaze grew serious. "Thank you. Thank you for giving me another chance. All the while I was driving up here, I thought I'd wake up in hell this morning, but here I am in heaven."

"Thank *you* for giving us another chance." Lauren lowered her mouth to Jac's and for long moments kisses spoke for them. With a happy sigh, she dropped her head back to Jac's shoulder and rested a hand on her chest.

"You never did answer me."

"Mmm?" Lauren was fascinated by how quickly Jac's nipples responded to her lightest touch.

"What were you thinking about so hard?" Jac squirmed, but made no move to stop Lauren's explorations.

Lauren's fingers stilled. *Ask her. No secrets, remember.* "I was wondering if you'd have gone through with it. If I hadn't shown up, would you have had sex with Victoria?"

"I never wanted to, not even for a moment."

"I know that. She said that you were punishing yourself for making the bet by paying up. I guess I'm having a hard time imagining you and her doing what you and I did together last night."

Jac sighed deeply. "I'm not sure what to tell you. Obviously I was prepared to follow through since I showed up here—"

"Toy bag in hand."

Jac winced. "True, but I also found the whole situation surreal. A big part of me didn't believe it would actually happen. When it came right down to it, if Vic offered me a last minute out, I'd have taken it...I think. All I know for sure is that I'm grateful beyond words that it was you here and not her."

"Huh."

"Please don't be jealous, especially of something that didn't happen."

"It scares me how close it came to happening; how close I came to not being with you this morning."

Jac tightened her embrace around Lauren. "That scares me too, but I'm here. You're here and Vic's not. That makes me ecstatic, grateful, relieved, optimistic—"

"So you're happy things turned out the way they did?" *Believe her. Believe in her.*

Jac laughed. "That is exactly what I'm saying. And you? Any regrets? I know we probably strayed well outside your comfort zone last night."

"I'm fine. Better than fine. I'm looking forward to today and tomorrow." Lauren shot Jac a grin and pinched her nipple.

Jac sucked in her breath. "I think I've created a monster."

Lauren deposited a kiss on the nearest bit of flesh and sat up. "Well, this monster has to use the facilities. Back in a moment."

While in the bathroom, Lauren took time to wash up and clean her teeth. When she was done, she examined herself in the mirror. *What did you expect? That you'd look different after last night?* It seemed as if such a life-changing night should be memorialized in her face and body, but her mirror image was unchanged.

She returned to the bedroom.

Jac smiled as she watched Lauren approach.

Well, this is one big difference. Lauren had never been completely comfortable with nudity around Phil. With Jac, she revelled in it. She leapt the last foot to the bed and pounced on Jac, pinning her under the covers as she straddled her. "So, long, tall, and sexy, what do you feel like doing today?"

Jac laughed as she struggled to get her arms out of the cocoon. "I believe that's not up to me, mistress. But if you would permit me to use the bathroom, your sub would be deeply appreciative."

Lauren pretended to think about it, then rolled off to the side. "Oh, all right. Just this once. But don't get used to it."

Jac clambered over her, stopping for a kiss on the way.

Lauren watched her walk to the bathroom and grinned. Jac's cocky little swagger was back. *Someone's feeling full of herself.*

Jac took her time, and by the time she sauntered back to bed, Lauren was growing impatient. *Someone needs a little reminder of our agreement.* "Come over here." She pitched her voice low and husky.

Jac's eyes widened and her lips parted.

"Now."

Jac hurried to Lauren's side of the bed.

Lauren laid a hand on Jac's thigh. "Turn around."

She did so and Lauren ran a hand over Jac's buttocks, tracing the lines she'd left there the previous night. "Do these hurt?"

"Not unbearably."

"I'm glad. Feet apart."

Jac separated her legs.

Lauren began a gentle exploration. *If she's as sore as I am...*

A shudder ran through Jac's body as Lauren teased her. Within a moment or two, her hand closed on the quilt, squeezing it in time with Lauren's movements. "Please..."

"Please what?"

"Please, may I lie down? I'm not sure my legs are going to support me."

Lauren kept her movements slow and light. "Not quite yet."

Jac sucked in a deep breath.

She waited for the sounds that told her Jac was on the edge and then pulled her hand away. "Turn around."

Jac turned, her chest rising and falling rapidly. "God, woman, you're killing me..."

"I suspect you'll live." Lauren pushed back the covers to expose herself and spread her legs. "You don't get to come to bed, or come, until I do."

It wasn't an optimum angle, but Jac threw herself into the task and, within moments, Lauren was thrashing under her mouth and scratching at her back as she climaxed.

She slumped back on the bed, and Jac stood erect with a satisfied grin. "You're looking a bit too pleased with yourself. Maybe I should keep you waiting a little longer."

Jac bowed her head, but her smile lingered. "I only aim to please, ma'am."

"Get your ass in here."

She dove under the quilt, covering Lauren's body with her own. Her eyes gleamed as she touched delicate kisses to Lauren's face. "Please?"

Lauren wrapped her arms around Jac's back and slid a thigh between her legs. "Please what?"

"Please, may I come?"

She dropped her hands to Jac's buttocks and thrust up with her thigh. "Yes."

As her hips moved faster, Jac pushed up on her hands and threw back her head. She came silently, her arms rigid and her neck extended.

Lauren gazed in awe. *She's so beautiful. She looks just like her statue.*

Jac slumped into her arms, and Lauren caressed her back as she waited for Jac to regain her breath. "I understand now."

Jac's breathing slowed. "Understand what, sweetheart?"

"To be able to arouse you to such a degree—to control your pleasure—it's intoxicating, isn't it?"

"Yes." Jac rolled to the side and put her head on Lauren's shoulder. "But don't think it's just because of the way we've made love. I've never mixed love and play this way. It is exhilarating, but it's intense because it's you and me, not because of toys or techniques."

"So Sous-terre isn't like this?"

"Not at all, though it's fun in its own way. If you want to see, I'd be happy to take you there some day."

"Maybe. I'll have to think about it."

"Okay. You're the boss."

Lauren kissed Jac's forehead. "Only for this weekend. Equal partners, remember?"

"I remember every word you've ever said to me."

"Somehow I doubt that."

"Test me."

Test her? Okay. "What was the very first thing I ever said to you?"

"You told me I was welcome to crash your birthday lunch and that you'd been looking forward to meeting me because Vic talked about me all the time."

"Mmm. I'll have to take your word for it, but it sounds about right. What did I say when you came out to me?"

Jac laughed. "You said you weren't bothered by it."

"And you said you wouldn't let my being straight bother you." Lauren lifted the covers to look down the length of Jac's naked body resting against hers. "Who knew, eh?"

Jac's chuckle rippled against her chest.

"Okay, here's a very important one—what did I say the first time you told me you loved me?"

"You said you loved me, too—but I think I should get dispensation on that one, because as I recall, I was coming down off the most magnificent orgasm of my life, so my memory might not be that accurate."

Lauren rolled Jac on her back and slid on top. "No, your memory is perfect. And I do believe a reward is in order."

"Have I mentioned that I really, really like the way you think?"

Jac carried the last of their bags to her SUV and grinned as she stored the toy satchel with the rest of their stuff. *What a weekend. And what an incredible difference from what I'd expected.*

Lauren stood on the porch, staring out over the valley with a smile on her face.

"Ready to go, sweetheart?"

"Almost. I kind of hate to leave and return to the real world."

Jac moved up behind Lauren and wrapped her in an embrace. "I know exactly what you mean. I'm thinking we might have to get our own home away from home one of these days, maybe at a lake or something."

"That would be nice, but nothing will ever be the same as our first time, will it?"

Jac nuzzled Lauren's hair. "Maybe not the same, but certainly just as wonderful. When all is said and done, as fabulous as this weekend was, we have so much more to look forward to." *Growing old with you, for one thing.*

Lauren turned and linked her hands behind Jac's neck. "We do, don't we? Have I mentioned recently how much I love you?"

"I do believe you were screaming that at the top of your lungs about an hour ago." Jac grinned. *God, you're cute when you blush.*

Lauren swatted her. "I wasn't the only one screaming."

"Agreed. It's a darned good thing Vic's cabin is so isolated, or someone might've gotten the wrong idea…especially if they'd seen the way you were taking advantage of poor helpless me."

Lauren snorted. "You're about as helpless as a lioness."

"And you, my darling, much to my surprise and delight, are no lamb. I'm going to have to wear long sleeves to the office tomorrow to avoid uncomfortable questions about exactly what I got up to this weekend."

Lauren grinned and took Jac's hand, leading her to the SUV. "Aw, my poor baby. Let's get you back to the safety of your lair."

"Our lair." Jac climbed into the driver's seat and started the vehicle.

Lauren fastened her seat belt and was quiet until they were out on the road heading down the mountain. "About what you said?"

"Mmm? About what?"

"Our lair. You know I have my own place, right?"

A bolt of alarm shot through Jac. "But, I thought—didn't you leave Phil's?"

"I did, and I'm never going back. But I rented an apartment last Monday and took possession of it on Friday."

Jac was quiet for a long moment. "I understand why you did that under the circumstances, but you do know you're welcome to live with me, right?"

"I don't think we're ready. For now, at least, I need my own space. I lived at home until I moved to Calgary, and I'd only had my own apartment for a few months before I moved in with Phil. It was a mistake, and I'm not going to make the same mistake with you. It's too important to me to get this right."

Jac's shoulders slumped. "I'm not Phil."

Lauren caressed the side of Jac's face. "I know you're not, and I don't want you to be upset about this, but I really think it's for the best. We're still going to see each other all the time—"

"For sleepovers?" *I want more. I want you with me every day.*

"Of course, among other things, but I want to build a life with you, and to do that, I need to know who I am. That means there are times I'll want to retreat to a quiet space. It doesn't mean I don't love you. God, I love you so much that I can't imagine my life without you."

Jac shot Lauren a smile. "That's the way I feel, too. I do understand and I'll give you your space, but I'm going to count the days until I get to wake up with you again."

"I'm going to count the days until I go to sleep with you—and the ways I can keep you from sleeping."

Jac laughed at the mischievous tone of Lauren's voice. "Good. I think we tried out everything in the toy bag, but there are always variations. I still have a few ideas."

Lauren squeezed Jac's thigh. "So do I."

When they arrived in the city, Jac followed Lauren's directions to her new home, where she pulled in behind the yellow bug. She jumped out and went around the back to get Lauren's overnight bag.

"Did you want to come in? It's a bit of a mess yet. I haven't really had time to settle in."

Jac shook her head. "Thanks, but I'm sure you'd like some time to get squared away." She leaned down to kiss Lauren and was pleased when the kiss was returned without reservation. "I'll call you later, okay? Or if you'd rather I didn't—"

"Call me," Lauren said firmly. She waved before climbing the stairs to the above-garage suite.

Jac waited until she was inside before she got back in the vehicle. She sighed and started it up. *This is going to be hard. I miss her like crazy already.*

On the way back to the loft, Jac stopped at a hardware store to have a copy of her house key made. *Should've hung onto Marc's instead of mailing it back to him.* While she waited for it to be cut, she looked over the selection of key fobs. A tiny pewter replica of a classic VW Beetle caught her eye. *Perfect.*

Once home, Jac started to tidy up. She didn't know how many days it would be until Lauren came over, but the past week of gloom and depression had not been conducive to good housekeeping.

She'd just thrown in a load of laundry when the buzzer sounded from downstairs. "Hello?"

"Hey there, long, tall, and sexy."

Jac grinned broadly. "Hey there yourself, short stuff."

"Going to let me in?"

"Hmm, well, I don't know that I should. I have a very demanding lover who might not approve of me allowing some woman off the street into my loft."

"Honey, you do know that the terms of our agreement aren't officially up until midnight tonight, right?"

"Well, when you put it that way…" Jac buzzed the door open and hurried down the stairs. She met Lauren on the second landing and swept her into a kiss.

"Mmm, I do like the way you put out the welcome mat."

Jac pressed Lauren against the wall. "The welcome mat is permanently out for you." They ran their hands over each other as if they hadn't seen each other in weeks, kissing all the while. When they finally came up for air, Jac asked, "Not that I'm complaining in the least, but what happened to 'I need my space'?"

"It occurred to me that I once heard a rumour that flannel sheets are wonderful to sleep in naked. Since I don't own flannel sheets and you do, and I have tomorrow off, it seemed to me to be the perfect time to assess the rumour for myself."

Jac laughed and drew back. "As it so happens, I just put clean flannel sheets on the bed so your timing is perfect." They walked upstairs hand in hand.

Back in the loft, Jac picked up the freshly minted key. "This is for you. I don't want you to think I'm putting pressure on you, or that I have any expectations. I promise I'll give you all the space you need, as long as you need it, but I wanted something to show you that I'm committed to us—to our relationship. I could say something corny about this being the key to my heart, but you've already got that. You had it long before this weekend, and I fervently hope you know that. This is just the key to the place that someday I hope you'll call home, too."

"That's so sweet of you. Thank you. I'll give you a key to my place, too." Lauren slipped her arms around Jac's waist. "Just so you know, I fully intend to join you here one day. And I appreciate you understanding my need to go a bit slower than you'd like. But for now, I want to make love with you in every corner of the home we worked on together."

Jac rested her arms on Lauren's shoulders. "Were you planning to hit every corner tonight?"

Lauren grinned. "Maybe not every corner. You displayed amazing stamina this weekend, but I don't want to push my luck. I have long-term plans for us, which means I can't wear you out all at once." She took Jac's hand and led her up the stairs. "Actually, I thought it would be a great idea to start with a bath in that marvellous tub made for two. I've been fantasizing about that since the first time I bathed there."

"You have?"

"Uh-huh."

"Seriously? You were really thinking about me that way back then?"

Lauren laughed. "Back then? It was only a few weeks ago, and yes, I may not have known exactly what was going on, but you excited me from the start."

Jac grinned. "Cool."

"This may sound crazy, Lord knows it does to me, but from the first day we met, I felt a connection. I was thrilled when you asked me to help with your place, because it gave me an excuse to see you. And even when our friendship made my home life more difficult, I could no more stop what was happening between us than I could stop breathing. I may not have understood it for a while, but it was real. It is real."

Jac caught her breath. "It is, and has been from the beginning. I hate the bet I made with Vic. You were right about me—"

"Shhh, the old you, maybe. But I not only love you, I really, really like the woman I just spent the weekend with. And I don't mean just the sex, though that was amazing."

"It was. You are."

Lauren took a step back and lifted her sweater over her head. She walked backward, peeling off her clothes and dropping them to the floor until she was nude. She turned, then stopped in the bathroom doorway and looked over her shoulder. "Coming?"

"God, yes!"

Epilogue

The lights of the Christmas tree reflected and refracted in Jac's crystal glass. She took the last sip and set it aside. *Mmm, a few of those will certainly add to the holiday pounds.*

"Would you like another?" Cynthia asked. "There's lots more."

"Thank you, but no. It was fabulous, though. I've never had homemade eggnog."

Lauren handed Jac her glass to set aside, too. "I could never drink store-bought nog after having Mom's all these years. I've been spoiled."

Jac tightened her arm around Lauren's shoulders. "Good. You deserve to be. And you will be, if I have anything to say about it."

Lauren patted Jac's belly. "You old sweet-talker. Hey, why don't we give those new skates of yours a workout?"

"Now? It's almost ten. Won't it be too dark out?"

"It'll be dark walking there, but we'll take a flashlight. Dad rigged a light with a generator for night skating, so we'll be fine."

"Okay then, let's go. Maybe we'll see Santa fly overhead."

Sara looked up from where she'd been scrutinizing the presents under the tree. "Can I come, too?"

Cynthia shook her head. "Not this time. I need your help to set out the Santa cookies." She winked at Jac and Lauren. "We'll let them go by themselves tonight."

"How about if we take you skating tomorrow afternoon?" Jac asked.

Sara nodded. "After presents."

Lauren laughed. "Definitely after presents, sweetie." She stood and extended her hand to Jac. "C'mon, you, we need to bundle up before we go."

They went to Lauren's old room to get ready. Jac sat on the edge of one bed to pull on warmer socks. "You know, I love coming up here, but do you think we can talk your mom into letting us replace these twins with a queen?"

Lauren smiled. "What? And miss the fun of stealing into each other's beds during the night?"

"Hah, fun for you, short stuff, but there's not a lot of room when a certain bed hog takes more than her share."

"I thought you liked close quarters."

"I do, but falling out of bed onto a bloody cold floor was not a lot of fun last night."

"You have a point, and I actually did talk to Mom about that this morning. I told her that since both Anjali and I bring our significant others home with us now, we'd really rather have one bed to share in our old room. She told me she's already thought about that, and she's just waiting for January sales to buy a queen-sized bed."

"I'd be happy to buy one for her."

"I know you would, but it's important to let her do it. She wants to make it clear you're as welcome here as Jeffrey."

I really like my hopefully future mother-in-law. "That is so nice of her."

"It is, isn't it? Of course, she has no idea what we might get up to in that lovely new bed."

"Lauren! Not in your parents' house."

"I'm pretty sure they know we sleep together, love."

"Well, sleep, yeah, but the bag stays at home."

Lauren's eyes gleamed, and she waggled her eyebrows. "No problem. I've learned to improvise."

"Tell me about it." Jac shook her head. *Who knew kitchen implements had so many other uses?* She stood up, pulled on her overcoat, and slung the skates over her shoulder. "Okay, I just need my boots, and I'm ready for our adventure."

"Good. I like you that way—ready for an adventure." Lauren preceded her out of the room.

Jac watched the sway of Lauren's hips. She was amused at the innuendo. *Someone's in the mood tonight. Reminder to self—your future in-laws sleep not that far away. Run silent, run deep.*

They left the house. Lauren's flashlight showed the way under a black sky blanketed with brilliant stars. It was cold, but there was no wind, and they enjoyed a peaceful walk across snowy fields.

When they got to the skating rink, Lauren started the generator and turned the overhead light on. Jac sat down on the old wooden bench. Lauren could skate rings around her, but she'd been practicing at a local rink on the few nights Lauren didn't stay with her and was eager to show off her improved skills.

By the time Lauren sat down to don her skates, Jac was on the ice. It wasn't nearly as smooth as the rink, but she did a decent impression of a basic spin before losing her balance and falling.

Lauren skated over and offered her a hand. "Hey, careful there, hotshot. I have plans for that body tonight. Don't break it. What do you say we try something a little easier, like skating hand in hand?"

Jac got to her feet and flicked snow off her clothes.

Lauren brushed vigorously at the seat of Jac's pants.

Jac peered over her shoulder and smiled. "Excuse me? I think I'm snow-free now."

Lauren grinned. "You never know. I might have missed a flake or two."

"I think the only flake is standing right beside me." Jac extended her hand, and Lauren took it. They skated around the circumference of the small area.

Lauren raised their conjoined hands. "I like it better when we don't have to wear gloves."

"I do too, but I think we'd freeze our fingers off."

"True, and I do have plans for those fingers."

Jac pulled Lauren to a stop and into her arms. "Does a certain someone have something on her mind tonight?"

Lauren lifted her face for a kiss, which became many kisses. "Your certain someone always has that on her mind. You should know that by now."

"I do indeed." *And thank God for that.*

They resumed skating; Jac tried going backward.

Lauren gave a small whistle. "You've really gotten better at this. Have you been holding out on me?"

"Nope. Just shaking the rust off. I haven't done this since I was a kid." *And no way am I telling you how many hours I've spent at the rink.* Jac executed a smooth half-spin to wind up back at Lauren's side.

When they came back around to where the generator hummed noisily, Lauren stopped. "Would you mind if I turned this off for a little while? I think there'll be enough light from the moon to see by, now that we've done a few circuits."

"Sure, go ahead. But if I take a header, I'll depend on you to nurse all resulting injuries."

Lauren glanced over her shoulder as she scrambled up the bank. "So you're saying you want to play doctor tonight?"

Jac laughed and the sound echoed in the still night. "You are incorrigible."

Lauren slid back down to Jac's side. "Phhsst. Talk about the pot calling the kettle black."

"We are a pair, aren't we?"

Lauren stood in front of Jac and took her hands. "A perfect pair, if you ask me. Would you mind if I give you two of your gifts right now?"

"You don't want to wait to be with the family tomorrow?"

"Not for these two."

Jac grinned. "Okay, but I know you. Keep in mind that any flesh we bare is going to get frostbitten really fast."

"We'll save the flesh baring for later, love. Actually, my first gift is a request."

"Okay. Anything I can give you is yours. You know that."

"It's a simple request. I'd like my spare key back."

Jac's face fell. "You do? Why?"

"Because I have to turn the keys back to the landlady when I vacate my place at the end of the month. Think you can put up with a new roommate?"

Jac bounced with excitement, and Lauren had to grab her to keep her from tumbling to the ice. "Oh my God, yes! This is the best gift ever! When did you...why did you...what took you so long?"

Lauren laughed. "When—probably two weeks after we got together at the cabin, I was ready to move in with you, but after making that big speech, I figured I had to save face and keep my apartment at least until the end of the year. Why—I'm at my own place so rarely that I'm sure my landlady thinks I'm a spy leading a double life elsewhere. And as to what took me so long..." She wrapped her arms around Jac and kissed her softly. "As sure as I was, I had to be absolutely, positively certain that you felt the same way."

Jac tucked some stray hairs back under Lauren's toque. "And now you are?"

"I am. These last few months, you've shown me in a thousand different ways that you're one hundred percent committed to us."

"I am." *Should I do it now? No. I think I'll wait for our first official night together at home.* "Thank you. You really couldn't have given me a more perfect gift. This is the best Christmas ever." Jac tilted her head down and kissed Lauren. Their cold lips warmed up rapidly.

Lauren laid a hand on Jac's chest. "I said I had two gifts for you."

"Nothing could top this."

Lauren's eyes sparkled in the moonlight. "Funny you should say that. I took the liberty of making New Year's Eve plans for us. I hope you don't mind."

"Not at all. Are we going out for dinner? A show? A tropical cruise?"

"Actually, love of my life, we are going out for dinner, but then we're going to bring in the New Year at Sous-terre."

Jac's jaw dropped. "You're kidding."

"No, I'm not."

"But I thought we agreed— I didn't think you wanted— I'm confused."

Lauren met Jac's gaze. Her eyes were serious and intent. "I know I said I didn't want to go, but it was a big part of your life, and if I'm going to share your home and life, as well as your bed, it's something I want to experience with you. I don't know if this is a one-time thing. I won't know that until after we go, but I do want to try it."

Jac nodded. "Okay, but I want you to know I'm completely happy as things are. I haven't been back to the club since our first weekend together, and I don't really care if I ever go again."

"I know. If I thought otherwise, I wouldn't be moving in. I always knew we'd find our own path, and we have, but I'm also curious. So let's put on our best dresses and see the New Year in with style."

"The club it is, then. But just so you know? You're not going to be in your dress long enough for anyone to notice."

Lauren laughed and brought Jac's hand to her lips. "I'll follow your lead, love…the first time anyway."

"Perfect."

About Lois Cloarec Hart

BORN AND RAISED IN BRITISH Columbia, Canada, Lois Cloarec Hart grew up as an avid reader but didn't begin writing until much later in life. Several years after joining the Canadian Armed Forces, she received a degree in Honours History from Royal Military College and on graduation switched occupations from air traffic control to military intelligence. Having married a CAF fighter pilot while in college, Lois went on to spend another five years as an Intelligence Officer before leaving the military to care for her husband, who was ill with chronic progressive Multiple Sclerosis and passed away in 2001. She began writing while caring for her husband in his final years and had her first book, *Coming Home*, published in 2001. It was through that initial publishing process that Lois met the woman she would marry in April 2007. She now commutes annually between her northern home in Calgary and her wife's southern home in Atlanta.

Lois is the author of four novels, *Coming Home*, *Broken Faith*, *Kicker's Journey*, *Walking the Labyrinth*, and a collection of short stories, *Assorted Flavours*.

Her novel *Kicker's Journey* won the 2010 Independent Publisher Book Award bronze medal, 2010 Golden Crown Literary Awards, 2010 Rainbow Romance Writer's Award for Excellence, and 2009 Lesbian Fiction Readers Choice Award for historical fiction. *Broken Faith* (revised second edition) was published in winter 2013. *Coming Home* (revised third edition) was published in spring 2014.

Visit her website: www.loiscloarechart.com
E-mail her at eljae1@shaw.ca

Other books from Ylva Publishing

http://www.ylva-publishing.com

Coming Home
(revised edition)

Lois Cloarec Hart

ISBN: 978-3-95533-064-4
Length: 371 pages

A triangle with a twist, *Coming Home* is the story of three good people caught up in an impossible situation.

Rob, a charismatic ex-fighter pilot severely disabled with MS, has been steadfastly cared for by his wife, Jan, for many years. Quite by accident one day, Terry, a young writer/postal carrier, enters their lives and turns it upside down.

Injecting joy and turbulence into their quiet existence, Terry draws Rob and Jan into her lively circle of family and friends until the growing attachment between the two women begins to strain the bonds of love and loyalty, to Rob and each other.

Broken Faith
(revised edition)

Lois Cloarec Hart

ISBN: 978-3-95533-056-9
Length: 415 pages

Emotional wounds aren't always apparent, and those that haunt Marika and Rhiannon are deep and lasting.

On the surface, Marika appears to be a wealthy, successful lawyer, while Rhiannon is a reclusive, maladjusted loner. But Marika, in her own way, is as damaged as the younger Rhiannon. When circumstances throw them together one summer, they begin to reach out, each finding unexpected strengths in the other.

However, even as inner demons are gradually vanquished and old hurts begin to heal, evil in human form reappears. The cruelly enigmatic Cass has used and controlled Marika in the past, and she aims to do so again.

Can Marika find it within herself to break free? Can she save her young friend from Cass' malevolent web? With the support of remarkable friends, the pair fights to break free—of their crippling pasts and the woman who will own them or kill them.

Walking the Labyrinth

Lois Cloarec Hart

ISBN: 978-3-95533-052-1
Length: 267 pages

   Is there life after loss? Lee Glenn, co-owner of a private security company, didn't think so. Crushed by grief after the death of her wife, she uncharacteristically retreats from life.
   But love doesn't give up easily. After her friends and family stage a dramatic intervention, Lee rejoins the world of the living, resolved to regain some sense of normalcy but only half-believing that it's possible. Her old friend and business partner convinces her to take on what appears on the surface to be a minor personal protection detail.
   The assignment takes her far from home, from the darkness of her loss to the dawning of a life reborn. Along the way, Lee encounters people unlike any she's ever met before: Wrong-Way Wally, a small-town oracle shunned by the locals for his off-putting speech and mannerisms; and Wally's best friend, Gaëlle, a woman who not only translates the oracle's uncanny predictions, but who also appears to have a deep

personal connection to life beyond life. Lee is shocked to find herself fascinated by Gaëlle, despite dismissing the woman's exotic beliefs as "hooey."

But opening yourself to love also means opening yourself to the possibility of pain. Will Lee have the courage to follow that path, a path that once led to the greatest agony she'd ever experienced? Or will she run back to the cold comfort of a safer solitary life?

Still Life

L.T. Smith

ISBN: 978-3-95533-257-0
Length: 352 pages

After breaking off her relationship with a female lothario, Jess Taylor decides she doesn't want to expose herself to another cheating partner. Staying at home, alone, suits her just fine. Her idea of a good night is an early one—preferably with a good book. Well, until her best friend, Sophie Harrison, decides it's time Jess rejoined the human race.

Trying to pull Jess from her self-imposed prison, Sophie signs them both up for a Still Life art class at the local college. Sophie knows the beautiful art teacher, Diana Sullivan, could be the woman her best friend needs to move on with her life.

But, in reality, could art bring these two women together? Could it be strong enough to make a masterpiece in just twelve sessions? And, more importantly, can Jess overcome her fear of being used once again?

Only time will tell.

Heart's Surrender

Emma Weimann

ISBN: 978-3-95533-183-2
Length: 305 pages

Neither Samantha Freedman nor Gillian Jennings are looking for a relationship when they begin a no-strings-attached affair. But soon simple attraction turns into something more.

What happens when the worlds of a handywoman and a pampered housewife collide? Can nights of hot, erotic fun lead to love, or will these two very different women go their separate ways?

Barring Complications

Blythe Rippon

ISBN: 978-3-95533-191-7
Length: 396 pages

It's an open secret that the newest justice on the Supreme Court is a lesbian. So when the Court decides to hear a case about gay marriage, Justice Victoria Willoughby must navigate the press, sway at least one of her conservative colleagues, and confront her own fraught feelings about coming out.

Just when she decides she's up to the challenge, she learns that the very brilliant, very out Genevieve Fornier will be lead counsel on the case.

Genevieve isn't sure which is causing her more sleepless nights: the prospect of losing the case, or the thought of who will be sitting on the bench when she argues it.

In a Heartbeat

RJ Nolan

ISBN: 978-3-95533-159-7
Length: 370 pages

Veteran police officer Sam McKenna has no trouble facing down criminals on a daily basis but breaks out in a sweat at the mere mention of commitment. A recent failed relationship strengthens her resolve to stick with her trademark no-strings-attached affairs.

Dr. Riley Connolly, a successful trauma surgeon, has spent her whole life trying to measure up to her family's expectations. And that includes hiding her sexuality from them.

When a routine call sends Sam to the hospital where Riley works, the two women are hurtled into a life-and-death situation. The incident binds them together. But can there be any future for a commitment-phobic cop and a closeted, workaholic doctor?

Coming from Ylva Publishing

http://www.ylva-publishing.com

Under a Falling Star

Jae

Falling stars are supposed to be a lucky sign, but not for Austen. Her new job as a secretary in an international games company isn't off to a good start. Her first assignment—decorating the Christmas tree in the lobby—results in a trip to the ER after Dee, the company's second-in-command, gets hit by the star-shaped tree topper.

Dee blames her instant attraction to Austen on her head wound, not the magic of the falling star. She's determined not to act on it, especially since Austen has no idea that Dee is practically her boss.

The Return

Ana Matics

Near Haven is like any other small, dying fishing village dotting the Maine coastline—a crusty remnant of an industry long gone, a place that is mired in sadness and longing for what was and can never be again. People move away, yet they always seem to come back. It's a vicious cycle of small-town America.

Liza Hawke thought that she'd gotten out, escaped across the country on a basketball scholarship. A series of bad decisions, however, has her returning home after nearly a decade. She struggles to accept her place in the fabric of this small coastal town, making amends to the people she's wronged and trying to rebuild her life in the process.

Her return marks the beginning of a shift within the town as the residents that she's hurt so badly start to heal once more.

Bitter Fruit
© by Lois Cloarec Hart

ISBN: 978-3-95533-216-7

Also available as e-book.

Published by Ylva Publishing, legal entity of Ylva Verlag, e.Kfr.

Ylva Verlag, e.Kfr.
Owner: Astrid Ohletz
Am Kirschgarten 2
65830 Kriftel
Germany

http://www.ylva-publishing.com

First Edition: October 2014 (Ylva Publishing)

Credits:
Edited by Alissa McGowan and Akilesh Sridharan
Cover Design by Streetlight Graphics

This book is a work of fiction. Names, characters, events, and locations are fictitious or are used fictitiously. Any resemblance to actual persons or events, living or dead, is entirely coincidental.

All rights reserved. This book, or parts thereof, may not be reproduced in any form without permission.